Howdy, Handsome

BY

CASSANDRA JOELLE

*"The whole earth is filled with awe at your wonders;
where morning dawns, where evening fades,
you call forth songs of joy."* Psalm 65:8

ROCKET LAUNCH SEQUENCE

CHAPTER 1: ANNIE

CRASH AND BURN

Early mornings at the ranch were my favorite time of day. The hustle and bustle that my chaotic life always brought me was still peaceful. The early, colorful sunrises brought warmth to the morning dew that slickened every surface. The last frost was nearing; I could feel it in my bones. We would have a warm spring, which was increasingly rare for this pocket of Wyoming that was known for its cold treachery.

My routine of drinking coffee with fresh cream and reading my devotional and Bible was cherished. Today, I took it to the front porch, where I had to be bundled in several blankets and the steam rose from my coffee in the cold air. The time outside made me feel closer to God. Connected to His creation. But I wasn't out there thirty seconds before the cows started mooing in the distance. The crowing from the roosters was next. A few *bahhhs* from the sheep let me know I needed to be better about tuning them out or go back inside. I never was good with distractions.

"Lord, if it is Your will, I pray that You send me a husband. I'm ready for love that honors and glorifies You. Amen," I prayed aloud, emphasizing every word.

Once my coffee was gone and my heart was filled with God, I pulled back my long, wavy, blonde hair into a low ponytail, put on my cowboy hat that doubled as my sun visor for the brightness that would inevitably swath this vast ranch, and threw on a thick pair of socks.

The first order of business was to feed the animals. I had ranch hands who would be arriving at any moment to help with the effort; between them, we usually had the task done quickly and could move on to the never-ending tasks of fixing fences, shoveling manure, and the general problem solving that running a ranch requires. Once the ranch hands got there, I took off with a snow shovel and hit the walkway of my small farmhouse.

Springtime at our ranch in Wyoming didn't mean tulips and flowers, but heavy heaping's of snow. Now, the weather patterns were changing rapidly, and I hoped that this would be the last of the snow for a while.

As I shoveled the walk around my home, I thought of my parents who passed down the ranch to me. Or, rather, I bought it from them, so they could finally live in their idea of paradise. It has been my father's family for over a hundred years, but my dad was never cut out for ranching. So, when I took a liking to the lifestyle as a child, he made sure I knew that it could all be mine when I was old enough to look after it. And the day I turned eighteen, he made good on that promise when he and my mother showed up with a moving van bound for the beaches of Florida.

Being an only child, I used to think I lucked out because I could take over the ranch. But now that I was twenty-six years old, single as it got, and my only relationships were those with the ranch hands and their families, I thought it would be nice to have someone around. Someone to talk to. Someone to work alongside with—to reach our dreams together.

For now, I didn't know what the end goal of ranch life was for me. I knew that I enjoyed this quiet lifestyle—I raised cattle, and my brand was highly sought after for its lineage, being one of the best known in the state. My herd was small but packed a mighty punch, as one of my steers at auction could sell for thousands and go on to start herds of its own. My sheep provided wool for two outdoor clothing brands that were based in Wyoming. My chicken eggs were sent to the diners in the nearest town, not that there were that many. God had provided for me. And yet, my heart yearned for a family. A husband. Children of my own.

Despite every grandmother in my church trying to pair me off with their "charming grandsons' that—spoiler alert, weren't so charming after all—I hadn't found anyone I would want to have a life with yet. I'd put my faith in God for Him to send the right man at the right time, and for now, I was waiting.

Unfortunately, the pastor at our church, John, took a leave of absence a few months ago and was currently in the hospital with health issues. While some were still meeting in small groups in their home, we did not have a community church right now which was my outlet in the past for meeting people. In my ranching community, it was made up of large acreages with just a handful of people living on each. I had twelve hundred acres. I lived in my family farmhouse, and there were some scattered cabins that the ranch hands lived in with their wives or small families. It was very remote here. I often laughed that I didn't know how God was going to send a man my way, but I did trust that He would when the time was right.

"Annie." Clint, one of the ranch hands who was also like a brother to me, called my name.

"Yeah?" I stopped shoveling for a moment, almost finished for the day. There were only a few inches on the pavement.

"A few head of cattle must have gotten out last night during that bizarre thunderstorm that brought this snow. I think we're missing three, and Jean said she hasn't seen Betty and her new twins yet. The numbers work."

"Was it the storm or were you playing with that karaoke machine again? You know they scare easily," I said.

"First of all, I'm an excellent singer. I just haven't found my audience yet." He put his hand to his chest like he was appalled. "Secondly, no karaoke last night. Jaylee's shows were on. I'm not allowed to make any noise when she's watching her shows." I laughed. These two seemed like the most ill-suited match that had ever happened in history but at the end of the day, Clint loved being bossed around. And in that sense, Jaylee was his soulmate.

"Okay, I'll go out and look for them. Thanks." I leaned my shovel up against the railing of my porch. "The amount of cattle that escaped here, you'd think we could be on *Prison*

Break," I mumbled under my breath. Looking back at my walk, the rest of it should have melted by the time I was back. I had an aversion to it turning to ice because here in this high-altitude climate, the ice would stay around longer than it should have and break every neck it came in contact with.

There were two full-time, on-site ranch hands, Clint and Trevor. The rest of our help came in seasonally, like when it was time to shear the sheep. Or if we had a lot of calves and did a large branding. We hadn't had one of those in years, as our angus operation had been smaller as of late, which was plenty manageable considering we had so many flocks of animals.

Last night's storm was loud. We hadn't had thunder snow in years. I nearly slept through most of it, but one particularly loud crash made me wake up. This morning, it looked like it didn't yield much snow, but more in certain swaths. It would be melted in an hour.

Saddling up my horse, Whisper, I gave her an apple that I grabbed from the kitchen on my way over. "We have a mission this morning. Remember that big, black angus cow, Betty? She had twin calves. They took off, and we need to find them." Whisper didn't react, but I had a strong bond with her, and I knew she understood. Whisper was a beautiful, white horse with a long, white mane, but had thick, black eyelashes. I got her at a horse sale when she was just a filly; she'd been with me my whole life.

The leather squeaked as I climbed into the saddle; the sun was starting to warm up the day, and I could no longer see my breath as it came out of my mouth. The snow from overnight began to melt, and the time I had before the frozen ground turned to mud was fleeting; springtime in the Rockies of Wyoming meant three seasons worth of weather every day. Whisper and I headed to the northern part of the ranch, where the cows might have fled to, as there was a flowing stream nine months out of the year and usually ample amount of grass. But right now, there wasn't much to eat or drink and with her young, it was imperative that I find them right away.

Turned out, Betty wasn't too far away, and she didn't put up a fight to return. In fact, once she saw me, she almost ran towards me, knowing there might be food involved in the rescue.

"Betty, what are you doing over here? You missed breakfast. Don't worry, we will still feed you but now, we gotta get all the way back." She didn't miss a beat, ambling towards me with her wide body that jiggled every which way, her twin calves following.

In the distance, I saw a large swath of white. First, I assumed it was snow, but there was also something in the center of it that was shiny. It was quite the distance from me, probably a half an hour ride there, so I decided to get the cows back to the ranch before I investigated further.

"Well, well, well," Clint said, crossing his arms at the caravan coming back toward him. "Someone had quite the walkabout?" he smirked, pushing a wheelbarrow of hay for the cows to eat.

"They were over by the well pump. Not sure what they would ever find more appealing over there when they have you pushing a wheelbarrow of food around for them right here," I smirked, taking the reins of Whisper higher in my hands, remembering there was something else out there that may have needed my attention.

"Annie?" Trevor, another ranch hand, called out as he ran over to me. I looked down to see him.

"Good morning—" he cut me off.

"Trish is in labor. Can I borrow your Ford? Mine is having that stick shift problem and—" I swiftly tossed him the keys from my coat pocket. "Thanks. I think I have better luck with yours not starting right than mine stalling out."

"Go. Be safe. I'll be praying!" I hollered, and he turned around and left on foot again as he ran back to his living quarters. They were only a hundred yards away, but Clint and I watched as if he might fall into a well or something on the way there.

"Wow, a baby is going to be born soon." Clint sounded joyful in his words, as I yearned to have the same experience. "I hope that car of yours makes it. I wonder why he didn't ask for mine?" Clint was just thinking out loud, and I scoffed. His truck had seats that looked like they were trimmed by a chainsaw. A puppy left unattended chewed through them years ago, and he never got around to getting them fixed.

"They probably didn't want to risk falling through the floor," I remarked, going back to my thoughts about the baby. "Thank You, Lord," I said, looking up to the bright morning sky, the brim of my hat blocking most of it. Whisper took a step into a sludgy part of the ground, and I was reminded that things were heating up quickly. "There's something I'm going to go check out about thirty minutes further North of the well patch where Betty was. Looks like a giant patch of snow."

"I hope it's not another mini glacier. Remember back in 2012 when that snow turned into a giant block of ice? The animals gravitated towards it like a satellite to orbit, becoming a giant salt lick. Your dad had to get that special industrial jackhammer to break it up, come June." We laughed at the memory.

"Man, I'd forgotten all about that. Those were the days," I said. I was just a kid back then, and my fascination with that mini glacier was on par with the animals. I, too, gravitated towards it.

"I'm getting back to it, then. Let me know if you hear anything about Trevor and Trish," Clint said as he headed back to the cows. "Do you have your radio on you?" Clint and I had decided since cell phone service on the ranch was nearly non-existent and only came if you were on the highest point standing on one foot with your tongue out and thumb in the air, we would get long range radios to communicate if there was an emergency or help was needed. I kept forgetting to carry mine, and I always seemed to be the one who needed help.

"Dang. I'll stop by the house and grab it," I said, regretfully pushing my quest out another few minutes.

"Okay. I got mine on." He patted to his belt., From it hung a radio, a cell phone in a holster, a knife in its sheath, and a small pistol.

"You got a can opener on you? I suddenly have the urge to open up some ravioli," I said, as Whisper and I hobbled around, trying to avoid the mud.

"As a matter of fact," Clint said with a proud smile, "this multi-tool has one. Wait. Are you joshin' me right now?" He gave me an annoyed look, and I laughed.

"Of course not. But the craving has passed. I know just where to look when it resurfaces, though," I laughed, heading straight for my house, which was just over a hillside. The cows could be heard from my porch and sometimes smelled. As I tore inside to grab the radio, Whisper waited patiently, her lead wrapped once around my porch railing. Finding the radio, I turned it on, saying a prayer of thanks that the battery wasn't dead in it since I never remembered to charge it, after all. Back outside, I climbed into the saddle and pulled left on Whisper's reins, gave her a gentle nudge to go, and we went riding into the distance.

Once I reached the well pump, I began to see the mysterious spot in the distance. From this angle, I decided it couldn't be snow because the snow on that particular hillside had already melted by the morning. It was facing the direction the sun rose this time of year and was usually the first to go. But if it wasn't snow, what could it be?

A few minutes later, when the bright red well pump was nearly out of my sight behind me, the wind changed directions. I caught a whiff of something that I didn't recognize. Fuel, maybe? I wasn't sure. Before I could decide, the wind changed again.

In Wyoming, the wind is always blowing. There's a long-running joke that if it stopped, we would all fall down. Up here in my parts, a normal day is between ten to thirty mile an hour winds. And that's just the breeze. My dad always joked that we should be kite makers instead of ranchers.

A scent hit my nose again as the shape became much clearer. It was a type of fuel. I slowed in my tracks; what was this? From here, it looked like the remains of a wrecked car. But there were no roads through here, and the ranch was fully fenced. I also didn't see any obvious tire tracks. For a vehicle to get to that spot right there and then somehow crash would be something for *Unsolved Mysteries* to decipher.

As Whisper and I got closer to the wreckage, I instinctively held my radio with one hand and the reins with another. Doing so made me feel that I could opt-out if things went south, which, running a ranch, it's not uncommon for something to go sideways, like riding a new horse. Or, rigging up equipment. You need to put safety above all else. And right now, I had no clue what this was.

"What in the. . . world?" The words slipped out of my lips like a prayer. We were mere yards away from it now, and I couldn't believe my eyes. "Is this a *spaceship*?" I nervously laughed at the thought.

Growing up, whenever a cow would break out and wander off, my father would tease me that aliens had abducted it. Later, when we would inevitably find the missing animals, I was always so relieved, and it was our long-running joke that some spacecraft in the night sky was after our cows. He was crazy for anything sci-fi and to this day, I was finding little green men figurines in the most random places. But right now, as I was seeing the parts and pieces of an oversized, larger-than-life crash that wasn't an airplane, those nervous feelings from my youth were returning.

Other than the wind howling in the distance, the site was silent. My hand went to my radio again before I remembered that Trevor was rushing his wife to the hospital, and Clint was tending to the animals. Without investigation, what could I even have said about this mystery site? Feeling my belt for my pistol—which every rancher keeps on them *just in case*— I dismounted from Whisper. I needed to see what this was.

The *object* was large, white, and partially flattened. The smell of fuel was overwhelming, and I was thankful for the wet, muddy ground, even though my boots were sinking a little with every step. It was lying on top of some sort of heavy fabric remnants that were ripped to shreds. After walking around half of it, I decided it looked like a dome, or rather, was supposed to. It reminded me of a cap on a plastic bottle. The middle of it hadn't flattened when it crashed. I pulled up my neck scarf to cover my nose; the smell was making me feel loopy. As I reached the other side of the object, something inside rattled and nearly knocked me off my feet.

A strange sound followed the noise. I looked all around me, in hopes that Betty had returned with lightning speed and walked another several miles just to see if I had hay in my pockets, but no—the sound was coming from inside the spacecraft.

Putting on my brave face—and the full armor of God in my heart—I said a prayer for protection under my breath and called out to the mysterious object.

"Hello? Is anyone there?" Pausing, I held my breath while I waited for a reply. My voice was so high pitched, I probably sounded frightened. Which I was. After a minute, I let out the breath I was holding, laughing a little while considering what my dad would say if he were here right now. "I come in peace," I said with a smirk. My dad had always been a bit of a dork for alien movies, and though I wasn't sure if anything like that existed, it was entertaining.

"Help." A male voice came from inside the craft, and I stumbled backwards, letting out a shrill from the fright. "Help, I'm trapped in here," the voice called out again. Putting all of my fear aside, I started running around the craft to see if I could find a way to get to the man inside.

"Is there a door or anything I can open from outside?" I hollered out.

"I… I don't know. I don't remember anything. I'm sorry." The man's voice was extremely apologetic.

"That's okay. I think I see something I can unscrew here…" I pulled out my multi-tool that was clipped to my inside jacket pocket and found the right tool that let me work on a panel that looked *almost* like it was supposed to be a door, when not smashed like a pancake. The first screw came out easily. *Too easily*—I had screws in my door hinges tighter than that—*no wonder this thing crashed.* The next five were another story completely, and it felt like hours had passed by the time I reached the last one. My upper lip was covered in sweat, and my jacket was tied around my waist as I wrenched my little tool in the screws. Finally, I was on the last one.

"Are you okay in there? I'm almost done, and I hope this frees you," I said, suddenly cautious about who could be inside. What if this was some experimental program from another country to rehome their worst criminals? I didn't detect an accent, but you never know.

"I think I'm unharmed. But I feel very weak, and I don't remember anything," the voice said back to me. He did sound weak. And no memory? What was this, an amnesia trope in a space man x cowgirl romcom novel? My aunt May was always reading far out novels with plots like this. I thought of calling her when I got home tonight to tell her as I twisted the last screw out. I smirked at the thought, while I pulled the metal plate as hard as I could. It didn't budge.

"If you are able—can you push on this panel? It's jammed from the crash, I'm guessing," I said, as I tapped on the door.

"I think I can—yes. Back up, and I'll try to kick it out," the man said. I stepped away, looking up at Whisper who was quietly grazing a few yards away. A loud kick came, and the panel moved a little, but didn't come open. Then again and again. A long pause followed.

"Are you okay?" I asked, worried about the answer and wondering what tools I could bring up here to rescue this man inside if this didn't work.

"I'm just feeling weak is all. I'm going to try one more time," he said, with defeat in his voice. I callled out to God.

"Lord—please help this man find the strength to break down this door!" After a moment of silence, a loud banging noise came from inside, and the door fell down. The man was freed.

I expected him to emerge immediately, but all I saw was darkness inside the craft. An uneasy worry took over my body—who, really, was inside? Was I in danger? Then, my eyes adjusted, and I saw the silhouette of the man: He was crouching and very banged up. He'd got cuts and bruises on his skin and tears in his flight suit. There was an American flag patch on his shoulder. His back was to me, the back of his suit reading *NebulaX*, which was one of our country's space exploration companies. It gave this man some much needed context and background, even if he couldn't remember that himself.

"Do you want to come out?" I asked the man, who seemed to still be gathering himself after the big door kick-down.

"Yes. . . I think I do," he whimpered. The craft wasn't tall enough to stand up in, in its current flattened state, so instead, he walked out on bent knees. His head was down, and I noticed he had a head full of lustrous, black hair. His bright white space suit with neon green trim was well- fitted, revealing he was quite in shape as well. When I realized I was looking this crash victim up and down, I was disgusted with myself. *Lord, please forgive me for checking this man out.*

As he stood up, I was greeted with his towering presence. Either aliens got better looking or I was having a daydream. The man looked like he was corn-fed in the best way. Even through his suit, you could tell he was ripped, which I didn't hate. *God, help me here!* But when he finally looked up at me and showed his drop-dead handsome face—the best-looking man I'd ever seen—the kind of piercing green eyes that could make me attempt to lasso Saturn if this was the kind of men orbiting it—

and a jawline that looked like it was forged from the steel of his spacecraft—I knew I was really in trouble.

"Howdy, handsome."

CHAPTER 2: JACK

A COWGIRL & A SPACEMAN

I didn't know where I was. Or what went wrong. Or, perhaps the most devastating, the question of who I was had seemed to evade my mind as well. I did know that this wasn't right. Something had gone terribly, terribly wrong. And the feeling of being late for something important was weighing on me heavily.

There was total darkness in here, other than the "Failure" lights that kept flashing inside my craft. As if I needed a reminder that this wasn't right. I didn't know how long I'd been here. The last thing I could recall was waking up in total darkness.

I was wounded. Not fatally, but the cuts on my arm and abdomen stung. My head was bruised; the soft spot on top of my skull made me wince just hovering my fingers above it. If only there had been someone I could call. But, without my memory, I didn't even know who I would ring or how I would do so.

When I closed my eyes, I saw a family. Was it my own? Perhaps. But in my daydreams, I was a child, running to my mother. There was another boy there with me, the same age as me perhaps. A father, too. We were all so happy. The boy and I played games. We were building a parachute to jump off the roof. We had a fort in the backyard. A tree swing that ran over a creek.

The love I felt for these people in my heart made me know that someone somewhere was out there looking for me, at least, I hoped. The longing I felt for them was undeniable. But the more I thought of them, the more I hurt. I needed to find a way out of this machine—and back to them. Back to my life. How did one go about remembering who they were? Perhaps, whoever had put me in this craft could help return me to them. That thought brought me comfort.

Though my mind did not remember, my body did, as I found myself flipping switches that detached the fuel load from my craft. I also opened the emergency vents for air. There was a supply of water and food in a cargo bin. Where did I learn this? I strained to think of anything other than the images of family in my head. For now, I was coming up with nothing.

After some time passed, not enough where I'd gone through my emergency water or had a meal, I heard a soft voice from the outside. There was a familiarity to it that I found comforting; could this have been someone I knew?

The woman was adamant on getting me out of this situation. I was eternally grateful for that, but upon trying to kick the door down, I realized just how very weak I was. I downed a bottle of water, to no relief. It may have been that my wounds were worse than I realized, or I was just that fatigued from the experience. I prayed it was the latter.

Prayer. I seemed to know what this was! God? "Lord?" I called out. Reconnecting with God would help me through this trial. I listened as the woman also called out to Him, asking for the strength for me to kick this door out. I echoed that prayer for a moment myself and gave the door one more try. God is good; I was freed.

Immediately after the door panel came crashing down, I was stricken with pain from the bump on my head. The bright light was blinding; I turned away from it. Shapes were swirling and the ground felt unsteady. I could never fully stand up inside this wreckage post-crash, but now I was down on my knees trying to regain my footing. *Vertigo.* I knew this feeling.

After a passage of time that I couldn't gauge, the woman invited me to come out of the craft. I opened my eyes to see the world had stopped swirling. Perhaps it was safe to do so? As I worked my way out, I took it easy. First, I ensured my feet were steadily on the ground. My eyes met the shoes of the woman; they seemed. . . western. I heard an animal *neigh* in the distance. The ground was damp and covered in prickly sagebrush, a stark contrast from my bright white suit. The land almost looked gray in comparison.

As I stood, I rubbed my eyes again before I could fully open and look up. They were still adjusting. I remembered something, but it was not important to my identity; I have light eyes—so light, in fact, that they could be sensitive. This fact was reigning true at this very moment. But when I finally stood up fully straight and looked out at the world around me, it was the woman whom I'd been rescued by.

The woman was the kind of beauty that makes the milky way look plain. All of the stars in the night sky were dull in comparison. In the universe, she was the sun—the brightest of all—and without her, nothing would have light. She was the most beautiful woman I'd ever seen and for a moment, I was lost in space.

Her high cheekbones had light freckling that reminded me of stardust, and her lovely lips pull me in like a black hole. Tumbling blonde hair, worn under a western hat. As our eyes met, the color was brought to her cheeks and also to mine. I felt like God was communicating with me, right here in this moment, but I didn't yet know what He was saying.

"Howdy, handsome. I'm Annie," she said, in a language that felt so foreign, yet I understood. Could it be that I was from here?

"Hi. I am... I actually don't know." Fear lingered in my mind, yet I knew that God was with me.

"That's okay. I see you are wearing a name patch on your suit. *Jack.* We will figure the rest out," she said, full of confidence. I winced again at the pain from my abdomen and head, my hands instinctively gripping my stomach. "Oh my," she said, pointing to my stomach. "We better get you to a hospital." Her eyes widened.

"I think it's just a surface wound. Do you have sutures? For some reason, I think I remember how to do those." I shook my head in confusion, which made it throb even more.

"Yes, in fact, we do. My mom used to be a nurse before she was a rancher. I have a whole closet of medical supplies back at my house," she said, her eyes squinting off into the distance. "I think I'll have you ride Whisper. Do you think you can be comfortable on a horse? You don't look well enough to walk."

A horse? I scanned behind me for the animal I heard in the distance before; she was a lovely animal but looked a little small for me. I felt too big to ride it and said so.

"Nah. You might be bigger than me, but um, you're pretty fit, if I say so. I appreciate that, but I don't think you weigh over 185. She could handle my father riding her, and he's about your size, so you're in the clear." I nodded, since I didn't have the energy to argue with that. And as I limped towards the animal, I was relieved to see she was much bigger up close, with her back coming up to my chest. As Annie helped me put my foot in the stirrups of the saddle, I looked down at the woman who had to be six or even seven inches shorter than me. How did she manage to get on this horse at her height? Annie worked fast to adjust the stirrups to my leg length and took the lead out of the saddle horn.

"I'm going to walk her, so you can just relax. Is it painful for you to be up there?" she asked, as we took the first few steps towards her house.

"Not particularly. I'll be okay. Thank you, Annie," I said, hoping to express my gratitude clearly to the woman who found me, while I tried to keep my overwhelming attraction to her at bay.

"You're welcome, space man. We will get you all fixed up and fed, and I bet you feel a lot better after that." The tone in her voice was caring; something that brought comfort to me. Comfort I was seeking. As the horse ambled strongly down the damp fields, with the sun working hard to firm up the muddy grounds of the vast, open lands, a question came to my mind.

"Where are we?" I asked. Annie smirked.

"Welcome to an unincorporated farming town of Big Horn, Wyoming. Population, *141.*"

"142," I said, with a wink. For as calculated as I felt, I was in my regular life; flirting with her was intentional. She smiled and her cheeks reddened at my gesture. The sun on my face felt rejuvenating, and I found myself wanting to close my eyes and stare up at it. But the moment I did, the images of the family came back to me.

This time, the mother and father were not there, and the boy and I were older. We were fixing up an old car and talking about our future. We both wanted to join the military service, but different branches.

As these visions flooded me, I wondered: Were these memories? Or from something I watched, like a show or a movie? No, not a movie. These things were *mine.* They were memories, and now, as I rode this woman's horse in a vast, foreign land of Wyoming, they were the only thing I had.

As we reached her home, which had to have been at least a two mile walk for her, I tried to apologize for requiring her animal to transport me. A woman should never have to take the strenuous way while a man sits in comfort, but every time I brought it up, she waved it off.

"Let's just get you back in one piece," she'd say, or "It's okay, Jack. I'm used to it." Used to what, exactly? Finding random crash sites around her ranch or giving up her pony for a man? I didn't like the thought of either. No, this woman I wanted all to myself. And those thoughts took me by surprise.

It became apparent that this was a large operation. There were cattle, sheep, and the clucking of chickens that just felt so out of place to me. I needed to get my bearings. I need to report to ground control. Wait!

"I know who I need to call," I said, as Annie patiently led her horse down the final stretch. She turned to me, smiling.

"Great! Who? I have a phone back in my house. There's no cell reception out here, so we are still using landlines." She pointed to the sprawling farmhouse.

"Ground control," I said, proudly. Her smile turned to a frown.

"Okay. I'm not sure they are listed in the phone book." She looked back ahead, and I saw a man, dressed in head to toe western, just like Annie.

"Is that your husband?" I asked. Annie's eyes widened.

"Clint? Oh my, no. We've known each other since we were in diapers. I would never…" She trailed off, laughing. "Clint is a ranch hand here. Well, he's so much more than that. He's like a brother to me. *An annoying brother.*" She laughed and shook her head. "He and his *wife* live on site in one of the other houses." I nodded. "I am single," she added in for clarification. My heart felt overjoyed at the revelation; like I could fly to the moon and back. Then the thoughts came rushing in: I wondered if I was single. I looked at my hands—no wedding ring. I didn't instinctively feel that I had a wife or children in the world.

Though I couldn't know for sure—it felt like the only family I had was my brother. I couldn't wait to find out.

"Well, well, well." The man, Clint, came over to us in a big hurry. "What do we have here?" He was smiling ear to ear and looking me up and down. Annie nodded, knowingly.

"Turns out that wasn't a giant ice lick. Seems we had some sort of crash-landing situation and didn't even realize it. Don't know how long he was out there, either, but I think he might have crashed last night during the storm. And... It appears he's suffering from amnesia." The longer she talked, the sillier I felt. I was at the mercy of strangers, without so much the knowledge of my own name.

"Is that so?" Clint whistled high and low and broke out into a laugh, slapping his legs with his hands. "If your dad was here for this! This might be the most exciting thing to ever happen around these parts! Annie, you're gonna be one of those social media stars." She shook her head.

"No, no. We are not going to exploit the situation for any gain, Clint. Come on." She shook her head but laughed with him.

"Yeah, you're right. Just can't believe this."

"Well, I better get him inside. He's wounded. I think some of dad's clothes will fit him," Annie said and walked us the rest of the way there.

The farmhouse was large. Big enough for a family. It had many gables with a wraparound porch that I imagined made for a great front seat to stargazing. Stars. Galaxy. Sky. Space. Wait a minute.

"I'm an astronaut," I announced, proudly. Right? Am I? I looked down at my clothes. They were a bit tattered, sure, but it was so obvious. Well, what else would I be? The disgruntled scientist who took a rogue flight on his own? One of those gamers who thought it would be the same as the flying in their games? Annie walked over to help me off the horse.

"I think you're right about that," she said. There was something else in her voice. Worry, perhaps? Anxiety? I had a feeling I had always been really good at picking up on these things. "Here, swing your leg over. Yep, good." It didn't feel unnatural for me to be riding this horse, but I was pretty sure the soreness to my legs let me know that I wasn't used to doing it recently.

Once I was back with my feet firmly planted on the ground, I felt dizzy again. Like I might fall over at any second.

Suddenly, the sky was spinning, and it felt like I was back in my craft, moments before it crashed.

"Let's get you inside, stat." Annie rushed me up the steps of her porch and instructed me to lie down on the couch inside the front door. She opened up the windows for some air while I immediately passed out.

*****

When I came to, Annie was standing over me. A fan was set up, blowing a nice cool stream of air onto my body but despite this, I was covered in sweat. Clint was sitting at the kitchen table.

"You talk a lot in your sleep," she said. I let out a grumble.

"Wh-what did I say?" I was eager for any pieces of the puzzle.

"Trajectory miscalculated. Booster separation failed... Cannot complete the mission." She spoke in a low tone that I gathered must have been an imitation of my own. I pondered if this cowgirl was the joking type, or if I really did sound that way when she said something else. "Hank, don't go." My heart dropped. A lump formed in the back of my throat. My chin started to quiver. I felt the feelings of sadness run through my body.

"Who is Hank?" I asked, not knowing the answer and not wanting to know. Whoever he was, my body reacted strongly to hearing his name. Annie and Clint had a look of concern on their faces.

"Let's focus on remembering who you are, and the rest will follow," she said, caringly. "And while we're taking care of you, let's get some of those wounds looked at." Annie sat down on the wooden coffee table that looked like it was carved out of a tree trunk, and Clint handed her a red bag. "Full disclosure—I've tied up some wounds after a dog got into it with a porcupine, but never on a person." Somehow, Annie's smile was all I needed to trust her. I'd let this woman do exploratory surgery on me if she felt it was necessary.

"I don't mind being the guinea pig," I chuckled, which hurt every bone in my body. Nausea was soon to follow. "I think I'm going to be sick," I whimpered, sitting up. The room was spinning even more.

"He might have a concussion, Annie. We shouldn't let him sleep," Clint said, voice full of concern. Annie nodded.

"I wouldn't call what he just did as sleeping. Other than him lying down with his eyes closed, his mind was on overdrive with all that talking." Clint nodded as Annie spoke.

"Would you like to show me your wounds?" she asked politely, digging through the first aid kit. I nodded as I tried to unzip the top layer of my space suit. After a few minutes of struggling, Clint stood up and walked to the front door.

"I can't do blood. Better get back to the cows anyway. Betty is probably planning her next escape while we speak. Nice to meet you, Comet Chaser." He grinned ear to ear at me and walked out. I had a feeling he wasn't the only other person I was about to meet here at the ranch. For as much excitement as Clint held about my situation, I think that word was about to travel faster than the speed of light.

Once I got the bulk of my gear off of my upper body, I was wearing the space pants and a thin cotton suit underneath. Just getting to feel the air on my skin made me feel eons better and the vertigo was passing. Suddenly, I realized how thirsty I was.

"May I have some water?" I asked. Annie nodded, pointing to the glass sitting on the coffee table next to her.

"I thought you'd never ask," she smiled. Annie had sparkling bright, blue eyes that rivaled the twinkling constellations that guided me home.

I reached for the glass and didn't put it down until it was empty. My thirst was far from being quenched. Annie was ready with a pitcher of ice water as she immediately refilled it. Two more glasses down did the trick. I didn't know if I could ever get used to her beauty, but writhing in pain certainly helped shift my focus from it.

We moved on to wound care as Annie cleaned the cuts and scrapes on my arms and even applied a small suture to one. I analyzed her work and was pleased.

"You're a natural," I said. Then it was time to look at the wound on my abdomen. I lifted up my shirt, and she went quiet. First, I assumed it was worse than I thought, and we were in over our heads. I groaned at the thought of needing to visit the hospital; I didn't know why, but I really, really disliked hospitals.

"Is everything okay?" I asked quietly, mentally preparing for her answer.

"Yep. I just need to clean this one, and you're right; it needs sutures." Relief washed over me.

"Great. Whatever keeps me out of the hospital." Annie started quietly working away, doing a wound wash and patting it with gauze. She applied almost no pressure to the area. I looked around the room as she stitched the skin back together; there was little sign of family in this house. She had a few knick-knacks sitting on shelves, a handful of colorful books, and a wool rug under the coffee table. A wooden cross hung at the door. No pictures of people anywhere. Log walls in this farmhouse. I wondered what her story was, and I felt myself longing to ask.

"Okay. You're all set," she said, eagerly jumping up from the coffee table where she had sat the whole time. I looked down at my stomach and saw a perfectly symmetrical line of stitching.

"Wow. Remind me to bring you some pants that need hemming," she smiled.

"I do sew and mend, so I guess this wasn't that hard after all. That is my favorite stitch pattern that you are wearing." Her laugh filled the room. "How about some food?" As she asked, I considered the fact that I didn't know the last time I had eaten anything.

"That would be nice. Thank you," I responded.

"Don't thank me yet. I'm not known for my cooking."

"Anything is better than what I have been eating." Annie looked over from the kitchen.

"And what is that? Are you remembering?" she asked. The visual of freeze-dried food took my mind captive.

"Yes, I suppose there are some details coming back. Like a rehydrated split pea soup. I'd give it zero stars."

"Yikes. That doesn't sound too appetizing. I don't think I could do it. If I don't get my steak and eggs, my body goes into a withdrawal." Annie put a cast iron skillet over a flame on the stove.

CHAPTER 3: ANNIE

SYSTEMS CHECK

If I had known that the Lord was going to send a drop-dead handsome space man my way today, I think I would have brushed my hair this morning. When this mystery man emerged from his craft, I had wild thoughts pass through my head. The first of which I had to stop myself from saying out loud, "Is that spacecraft from heaven?"

If Jack wasn't so darn attractive, I might have had more wits about me. All those feelings of keeping my radio on and my pistol at reach went out the window. I prayed that meant the Lord gave me discernment over the situation, and this man was harmless. Nevertheless, we needed to tread carefully. We didn't know anything about him.

His suit was like seeing something out of the sci-fi movies my dad liked to watch. It was like a classic astronaut suit, but also futuristic. The boots were more like a work boot shape, and not like something he'd be bouncing around the moon on. Which was a good thing, when it came time for him to ride Whisper. I didn't know how he'd get in the saddle if he couldn't put his feet in the stirrups.

As I walked back to my house with my mystery man, Jack, in tow, I felt waves of excitement rush through my body like adrenaline spikes. He must have crashed during the storm last night. I thought back to the loud *clap* that woke me—it was louder than the rest. Of course, I never would have imagined it was a literal *spacecraft* crashing into my ranch. Once Clint came into view, I knew there was some serious explaining to do.

The man crashed hard into the couch once we got him inside. I thought he was going to fall right into mine and Clint's arms before that. Thank You, Lord, for the strength to get him in.

The space man sure did say a lot in his sleep. So much so that Clint actually got up and made himself some popcorn, after asking permission to use my air popper. I gave him a look of steel, but he did it anyway. Clint has always been like a brother to me—full of sarcasm and loyalty, and neither of us ever avoided telling it like it is.

"What are you going to do with him?" Clint asked me, while the man was still sleeping.

"I don't know yet. This morning, it was all I could do to wrangle the stray cattle. Now, I have a stray astronaut." I put my head in my hands.

"We could call his company," Clint suggested.

"I thought about that but. . ." I trailed off.

"But, what?"

"But I don't know. Something doesn't sit well when I consider that." Clint raised his eyebrows. "Okay, fine. Do you remember that story like ten years ago about those monkeys that escaped a science facility?" Clint nodded.

"I don't know where you're going with this Annie. . ."

"I have a point; I promise. Okay. So, the monkeys get out. A passerby finds them miles away, on the run, and captures them. Returns them. They were momentarily free and wham— back to the lab."

"Is this man the monkey in this scenario?" Clint squinted his eyes and scratched his head.

"Sort of. My point is, we don't know anything that happened yet. What if he was on some sort of mission that he aborted on purpose? It's possible." I shrugged my shoulders.

"It sounds like you've given that a lot of thought, Annie," Clint laughed.

"I'm just leaning towards letting him recover first, before we announce anything. Besides, any spacecraft should have some sort of tracker on it, right? *'They'* probably already know just where he is. If this is anything like the movies, I expect them to show up on my porch any minute now."

"If I see two men in all black suits pull up, right before they wipe my memory, I'm going to say that you were right." Clint leaned over and razzed my hair. "Can I at least tell my wife? We don't keep secrets." He crossed his arms.

"Yes, of course. But tell her to keep it between us, please." Clint nodded.

"I'm serious, Clint. They don't call Jaylee the 'oracle of Big Horn' for no reason." I stared at him.

"You sayin' my wife is a gossip?" He put his hands in the air.

"No, I'm not sayin' that at all. I'm sayin' that when people want to know something, they ask her because they know that she has the information. She's like a library of local knowledge. This catches wind and.."

"Alright, alright. But don't go pretendin' that you don't ask her about every travelin' ranch hand that you see working the neighboring ranches," Clint said with a smile.

"Okay, okay. I'm just as guilty as the rest of 'em," I said with a laugh.

"You know. . . I think he's about your age," Clint said with a smile.

"*Ha ha.* I might be lonely, but I'm not going to *keep this man as my prisoner to marry him*, lonely. Besides, he might already be married. We don't know anything about him."

"That's a fair point. I would just assume even astronauts wear wedding rings," Clint said.

"He could be engaged. He could be about to pop the question. He might have a longtime girlfriend who is just dying to know where he is right now, crying herself to sleep."

"Is your Wi-Fi on?" Clint asked, pulling out his phone.

"Uhh. . . I think so. Why? You better not be doing one of those social media videos!" I gave him the look of death.

"Nah, nothing like that. I was thinking. What if we do one of those image searches? You know, of his face. You'd think there'd be something online about an astronaut, right?" Clint had a great point.

"Sure. Normally, I'd say get permission first, but I think these circumstances warrant taking action." Clint nodded and stood up, quietly walking over to him and snapping a picture.

"Darn," he said.

"What?"

"No results. I think we need his eyes to be open." For a moment, I let myself remember his piercing green eyes. They were so light, almost colorless.

"That's okay. Let's try again after he sleeps this off," I said, right before the talking started again.

"Hank, don't go. Don't leave me. I can't go on without my brother. I can't bury another person." Sadness filled the room. This man had experienced loss in immeasurable ways. It was sobering to hear. Clint put his phone away.

"I think you're right, Annie. We just need to let him rest up here with some privacy. Let's not tell anyone about this until we know what happened to him." I nodded and we waited for the man to wake up.

*****

When he finally came to, I knew we needed to address the wounds. Clint stepped out; he was the only ranch hand I knew who got queasy at the sight of blood. I used to tease him when I was younger when I had a scraped knee or a papercut, but now, he just walked away, which was fine. But I wasn't prepared for the feelings that came when I was alone with the man.

Lord, here I have a crash victim, bleeding on my nanna's old couch, and I nearly passed out myself when he showed me his perfect abs. Please, Lord, keep my thoughts pure and the temptations away.

When I was done stitching him up, I needed to walk away. I felt a magnetic pull to him that rivaled that of our solar system-—was this because he was gorgeous, and I was lonely? Or was it something else? Something predestined by God? I needed the headspace to pray, and I was having a hard time thinking clearly enough to ask God while I was still in eye contact with this man's perfect muscle structure.

As I chopped up some onion, sliced up a steak, and cracked a few eggs, my eyes kept wandering over to my mystery guest.

"I know you don't remember, but is it okay if I call you Jack? Because right now in my head I'm calling you *'Space Boy.'*" He cracked a smile as he downed another glass of water. *Perhaps I should call him 'Camel Boy' instead.*

"Sure. Maybe hearing it will help me remember."

"I think the name suits you," I said, turning to him and letting myself fully take in his appearance. It felt indulgent to look at him. You could just tell he worked out a lot. He was strong, with long, strong arms and legs. He was built tough. If he grew up here, he'd be a cowboy naturally. That I could see. His light green eyes had a twinkle to them that reminded me of the starry sky.

You could also tell that he was sensitive. There was a stillness to him, a sadness that was revealed to me which felt like a secret. One that even he didn't know. Just remembering that, I felt guilty for not telling him the whole truth of what he said. But deep down, I didn't think it was time for that.

"Really?" he asked playfully, interrupting my thoughts.

"Yes. You look like a movie star playing an astronaut."

"I'll take that as a compliment." He scrunched his nose and leaned back his head.

"I think you need to call Ground Control. Let them know I'm here. To come get me and my craft," he said, with a look of growing concern on his face.

"I just thought, maybe we should wait until your memory comes back. I mean, you can leave whenever you want, but would a few days' rest be all that bad?" Wait—was I keeping him here hostage? Was this turning into a hostage plot, or was I truly concerned for his well-being? He pondered that for a few minutes and relented.

"Yeah, I think you're right about that. Besides, I don't even know the company I work for."

"Well, that part is easy!" I called out, pouring the eggs into the pan with the now seared steak. "It's written on your back. It's quite torn, though." I watched him as he peered over his shoulder, as if he could read it. "Would you like to shower and change your clothes? My dad still has some things here, and I think they may just fit. He is tall like you."

"I would like that. Do I have time before the food is ready?"

"Sure. I'll keep it warm. The bathroom is just down the hall. I'll finish this up and put some clothes outside the door for you. I'll be on the front porch when you're done." He nodded and got up, both of which looked painful for him to do. I plated a heaping portion of the steak and eggs, poured a large glass of orange juice, and set it on the table.

Walking into my parents' bedroom was reminiscent. I hadn't been in here much since they left, and it brought unexpected sadness. I missed them, but it was more than that. Right now, if my dad was here, he would know just what to do. Honestly, he would be more excited about this than Clint. And he would have the best advice for what to do next with Jack. But since he wasn't here, I didn't know that I could call him and tell him. This felt like the type of situation where you have to be here to understand it. If I called and said, 'Hey Dad, a spacecraft crashed here last night. A lone astronaut was inside. He's wounded and has amnesia. Can he borrow your clothes?" My dad would probably be on the next flight. Of course, he'd still have to rent a car and drive three hours to get here from the closest airport. Our remoteness bought me more time.

Instead of calling my dad, I decided to wait. Clint was here. We had it handled. I found some newer jeans that looked like they would fit Jack decently. I found the rest of the clothes he would need and picked out a long sleeve button up that was green because selfishly, I wanted to see how much it made his eyes stand out.

The shower was going full blast while I left the clothes outside the door. My heart beat fast as I heard him moving on the other side of the door. I quickly turned on my heels and went to the front porch, like I said I would. Before I closed the front door, I heard the shower turn off.

Clint was out in the cow pasture, tending to some fencing. When he called me on my radio, I nearly jumped out of my skin.

"Earth to Annie," the radio screamed at full blast. I turned it down to an appropriate volume.

"Yes, Clint?" I said, with a snarky tone in my voice.

"How's Astro-flop?" I looked behind me, into the window of my home. The clothes were missing from outside the bathroom door. I expected him to emerge at any moment.

"You mean Jack. And he's about to eat." Clint reported back with laughter.

"That poor man has been floating around in outer space, crashes onto a cattle ranch in the middle of nowhere, Wyoming and now has to eat *your cooking?*"

"Har har," I snarked. "Got anything important for me, or are you just popping up to tease?"

"Nah. Just know that I'm here if you need me."

"Thanks," I said, peering back into the house as the gorgeous man, dressed in full western wear emerged. My heart skipped a beat. "Clint? One more thing. He's going to be wearing my dad's clothes until further notice. You might not recognize him." I turned my radio off as I went back inside to see if he needed anything else. You know, hospitality.

"Hey," I said, trying not to cause a scene over his new look. Sure, he was handsome as an astronaut, but this was over the top. "Here's your food," I said, pointing at the plate. His eyes brightened.

"Ah. Thank you. I tell you what, I feel like a new man after that shower. Thank you for the clothes, too. Your dad is pretty close to my size," he said, motioning to his pants that came up just a few inches too short.

"Oh, no. I may be able to shorten the hem on jeans, but so far, I haven't figured out how to perform miracles that would fix that," I laughed, as I spoke about his slight highwater jeans. "What size shoe do you wear? The right cowboy boot will fix that problem," I said with a smile.

"Twelve," he said with a deadpan as he bit into his food.

"Hey, Rain Man. Want to channel some of that memory for other parts of your identity?" I crossed my arms.

"Maybe the trick is to just answer before I think about it."

As he sat down at the table, he paused.

"Is everything okay?" I asked.

"Yes. I think there is just something I normally do before. . . Eating." I felt a pang in my heart.

"Do you pray?" He looked up at me in wonder.

"Yes. That's it. I'd like to pray." I nodded, and sat down, joining him in prayer. Afterward, he took a few bites. "This meal is delicious. Thank you, Annie, for taking care of me." He looked me in the eyes for longer than I knew what to do with. Suddenly, I had to get some water and open another window.

There is something so attractive about a cowboy. If I didn't know any better, I'd say that this one, sitting at my dining room table, was born and raised on a ranch. He certainly was looking the part. But today, I learned that astronauts are even *more* attractive to me. I guess I have a whole new type of man.

"I think that was the best meal I've ever eaten," Jack said, pushing his plate away as Clint walked through the door.

"Now I know that man has amnesia," Clint said.

"Very funny," I said in a dry tone.

"Trevor just texted, and I happened to be close enough to pick up your Wi-Fi signal to get it. It's a boy." He turned his phone to show me a picture of a beautiful, newborn baby.

"Wow. Already? And a boy! What a blessing." I took the phone to get a better look. "What did they name him?" I asked.

"I pushed for *Galactica,* on theme with today's happenings, but apparently James is a family name."

"James Ridge. What a great name." I handed the phone back; the perfect newborn engraved in my mind. I couldn't wait to have a family of my own.

"So, Jack. What's the plan for you tonight?" Jack looked at Clint and then back at me.

"I'm at the mercy of you guys. I have a mattress pad in my craft if I can get back over there, and I don't mind sleeping outside either. . ." he trailed off.

"That won't be necessary, bud. Lord knows you've been through enough. I think your options are my spare bedroom, or. . ." Clint trailed off.

"Or, what?" I gave him a sharp look. I knew he couldn't sleep here, but I wasn't about to let him sleep in the horse corral, either.

"What about that little cabin in the back, Annie? No running water, but I think he could handle it." I nodded.

"That's your first good idea in years, Clint."

"Glad to hear you're finally appreciating my level of intelligence. Alright, I'll go scare all the critters out of it. Where's that fly swatter?"

"I haven't seen it since you borrowed it last summer when you were having a particularly bad fly invasion. That's what you get for having too many horses wander over to your house. You need to stop giving them so many carrots," I said, cocking my head.

"Oh, that's right. In that case, we need a new ranch fly swatter. That one is severely damaged. I had to revert to the shotgun." Clint shrugged his shoulders. "As for the horses- they might get carrots, but they wander over because they *love* me."

"Empty your pockets—I bet you have some carrots in your jacket right now!" Clint put his hand over his left vest pocket that was bulging with something orange in plastic.

"Whatever. Okay, I'll be back, *Jack*," Clint announced, smiling at his rhyme.

"Sorry about that. Like I said, Clint is like a brother to me, and we argue like a couple of old maids," I said to Jack, turning my attention back on him. He just smiled.

"It's nice, actually. I have a brother, so I know what that's like." My face felt like it turned to stone.

"Look who's remembering!" I said, giving him a cheesy thumbs up. Maybe his sleep talking was that of nightmares, and his brother was still alive? *Lord, please protect this man's heart from the pain and anguish of grief.*

"Yes, things are slowly coming back, I think. I just need to focus on them. My brother, Hank—he's probably waiting for me." My heart felt like it dropped in my chest.

"I bet he is," I said, walking over and putting my hand on the back of his. Clint walked in during this emotionally charged moment, ruining the ambience.

"Well, the cabin is ready. Come on, *Apollo.*" I gave a look of steel to Clint, and he smiled and put his hands up in forfeit. "What, no nicknames allowed either? Sheesh," he said, laughing. Jack got up, his hand pulling away from mine, and slowly walked to the door.

"Wait—I forgot the bedding," I said, turning on my heels and walking to the linen closet. I grabbed a set of sheets and a quilt that my nanna made several decades ago. It was covered in quilted star shapes. How fitting for the astronaut. "Here you go," I said, handing it to Jack who stretched out his arms.

"Thank you, Annie." His eyes held my gaze for a moment longer than they should have, but I didn't drop mine either. Clint interrupted by clearing his throat.

"Let's go, Space Ace. My wife is making meatloaf and if I'm late, I don't get seconds. You think that I'm joking, but she's a really tough nut to crack, that one. It took me twelve months just to convince her to go on a first date with me. Another twenty-four months to get her to marry me. And still, I'm dancing on the edge even after marriage. So c'mon, buddy. Maybe I can sneak out the leftovers—give you some real home cookin' to experience." They started to walk out.

"I am quite tired, though it still feels early," Jack said, looking like he might pass out again.

"You better get some rest. I'll see you tomorrow," I smiled and waved goodnight.

As soon as he was gone, I released a deep breath and fell onto the couch. My mind needed to reflect, and my best reflection was time I spent with God. *Lord, what a day! You never cease to amaze me at the beauty of Your creation. Yes, Jack is so very handsome, but Lord, I want to pray for his mind. His memory is being returned to him in pieces, and I'm afraid that he's going to be in a very dark place when it comes back fully.*

Lord, be near to him! Bring him peace and comfort. And I pray that we do what is right in this situation. Whether that means calling his company or just laying low, please give me the wisdom I need to make the right decision.

It was not lost on me that I had been praying for God to send me a husband, and today, a man crash landed on my ranch. For a moment, I considered praying that he was not already married. But my heart was weary. If he had someone he loved, I didn't want to stand in the way of that. I had to remind myself that he was a stranger; I hadn't even gotten to know him yet! *Lord, please remind me that looks are not everything. Yes, it appears he's a godly man of faith. Yes, he's the most handsome man I've ever seen and yes. . . I can see myself falling for him. Please protect my heart if this is not for me.*

As night finally rolled around, the darkened sky was clear and filled with more stars than I'd ever realized. The air was crisp still, but nothing I couldn't handle with a thick blanket. As I took to one of the rocking chairs on the porch, I looked up at the sky with wonder. These lights, all placed by the Lord, shine down on us. I was reminded of a verse from Psalms 147:4, "He determines the number of the stars and calls them each by name." I was once again humbled by God and His magnificence.

And the same God who calls each of these stars a name, that I could only wonder what beautiful names they are, also created me. The same God who created Jack. As I sat there on the porch, basking in the light of the night sky and the beauty of His creation, I rested in the peace that God was working in my life and whatever the outcome of this situation, He was working all things together for good.

CHAPTER 4: JACK
ALL FLIGHTS GROUNDED

The cabin was small, but homey. It reminded me of something. Perhaps a memory from childhood. As I put the sheets on the bed, I tried to lean into it, but I couldn't remember. Yet. "God, please help me with my memories," I called out, as I prepared for sleep.

There was a small lamp on a desk with a rickety chair that looked like it might self-destruct if I sat on it. Other than the bed and a chair on the small cabin porch, that about made up all of the contents. Above the bed, a wooden cross hung on the wall, which brought me a feeling of overwhelming peace.

Without my memory, without my knowledge, there was only God in my mind. I longed for Him. I also longed for my family. My brother. My heart sought God and my brother relentlessly. "Lord, wherever Hank is, please let him know that I am okay," I prayed, as I kneeled at the foot of the bed.

My eyes felt heavy and my body dizzy. I needed a restful slumber so my wounds could heal. So that my mind could regenerate memories. So that I could think clearly. And yet, I wandered to the small front porch of the one room cabin and looked up at the sky as I relished in the wonders of the universe.

*****

A rap at the door woke me out of my deep, dreamless sleep. As I sat up, disorientation took a whole new meaning. Where was I? Who was I? Still wearing the undershirt from yesterday, I wasn't about to answer the door just wearing this and my shorts. So, I put one foot in front of the other and slid back into the jeans that were slung over the desk chair.

"Good morning." Annie gazed up at me from the small porch. Her eyes were glued to my face as I stood before her. "I thought you might like some coffee." She reached out a mug of piping hot liquid to me. I accepted, nodding and saying a groggy "thanks." Her eyes were as bright as the morning sun and her freckles that reminded me of a spray of stars looked extra beautiful. Annie was the kind of beauty that could turn dark matter into daylight. A small amount of shiny glitter was on her lips. I wondered what it would be like to kiss her.

As soon as the thought crossed my mind, I asked God for forgiveness. What if I was already in a relationship? *Lord, I feel like I'm single. But forgive me for overstepping here when I do not know for certain.* I let out a sigh, taking a drink of the coffee while Annie waited expectantly, as I struggled with the gravitational pull I felt towards this woman.

"It's wonderful. Just how I like it. Thank you," I said. Annie beamed a beautiful, perfect smile.

"You're welcome. And there's breakfast back in my house. One more thing," she said, pausing. "Clint and his wife would like to join us for dinner, if you are feeling up to it, that is. I don't know what your plans are. Of course, you don't have to stay here if you don't want to." She looked down.

"I would like to stay here while I figure these things out, if it's not imposing on you to do so. I do not want to overstay my welcome," I said, thinking it through for the first time. She looked excited to hear that.

"Great! We would love to have you. Well, come on by whenever you're ready to eat." She spun around on her heels and left.

As I dressed back into the long sleeve shirt she gave me yesterday, I had a nagging feeling that I needed to call someone. Obviously, I was expected to be somewhere—they don't just send out spacecrafts with astronauts inside of them without ever expecting to hear from them again, so that was clear. But it went deeper.

As I drank the coffee and prepared to go to Annie's house, I sat in the feeling for as long as I could, waiting for something to return to my memory. When nothing happened, I accepted my fate and left to see the beautiful woman next door.

The air was still crisp, but it felt good on my skin. The sky was bright. In this part of the Northern Hemisphere, I was guessing it was about eight in the morning. When I reached the screen door, Annie stood up from the table and waved me inside.

Annie's kitchen table was covered in food. Steak and eggs were on the center platter. A plate full of pancakes lay beside it, along with bacon that was still sizzling, and fresh fruit that had been chopped up. It was like a hotel buffet table but so much better, because it was in front of me right now, and I just happened to be starving.

As we ate, I asked her to share things about life here on the ranch.

"What do you want to know?" she asked.

"I don't know. I suppose I'd like to know what it's like to live out here, so remote. You're all alone," I said, biting into a heaping mound of pancakes.

"No more alone than you were in that spacecraft, floating all around the galaxies," she quipped.

"To be fair, I don't know where that thing took me or was planning on taking me. But I don't think I got very far. . ." I trailed off.

"Yeah, you're probably right. Still pretty cool though," she said, stabbing her fork into a piece of fruit. "Life out here is just what it looks like: raising animals, a little farming. We grow alfalfa. Clint wants us to lease one of our fields to sugar beet production. Trevor, whom you haven't met yet, his wife just had a baby yesterday. I know Clint and his wife want a lot of kids. So, I'm guessing in a few years, this place will be more populated." She chewed the strawberry and looked off into the distance.

"And what about you?"

"I would love to have a family. I just have to find a husband," she said with a laugh and wide eyes.

"That's not entirely what I meant but thank you for sharing." I was holding back my laughter. "What I meant was, what is your life like out here? Are you happy?" She pondered the question for a minute or so before answering.

"I love the ranch. I love Wyoming. I have visited bustling cities and big towns before, and I feel claustrophobic and like the noises are going to make me go crazy. This place equals peace for me. I feel God here more than anywhere else. But that doesn't mean it's not a little lonely sometimes."

"I think I know what loneliness is," I said, putting my fork down. "That feeling seems to be here with me, like a ghost." Annie had a sad look on her face while I spoke, trying to pinpoint the emotions that surrounded me. *Lord, help me.*

"Jack, there is something I should tell you," Annie said in almost a whisper. My eyebrows raised and Clint burst through the door.

"Who's up for an extra special mission today?" Clint asked beaming, his hands on his waistline.

"Read the room, Clint," Annie said, rolling her eyes and standing up. All was lost when I heard the word "mission."

"What sort of mission?" I asked.

"Look, Annie—his eyes are just sparkling at the idea of getting out of here!" Clint came over and playfully tousled my hair. Suddenly, I felt very concerned at how Annie might be feeling.

"No, not getting out of here," I said, as firmly as my voice could muster. I downed the rest of the glass of orange juice and stood, feet still a little wobbly.

"He's not sparkling, Clint. He's got vertigo. Possibly a concussion. And yeah, what mission are you talking about? Is there a sale on those tacky shirts you wear down at the feed store this morning?" Clint looked down at his button up long sleeve shirt that had plaid, paisley, and cows.

"My wife likes these shirts on me. My arms are longer, and I have a hard time finding anything else that fits right. And no, they are actually on sale all year long." Clint crossed his arms, turning back to me. "We need to go cut the fuel lines to that craft of yours, buddy. Lightning in the forecast today, and we can't let that thing set our whole field ablaze. We should also dig a fire line around it to prevent a fire from spreading, if it does light up like Nanna's Christmas tree the year she felt nostalgic and used real candles like her childhood." Guilt panged my heart. Cutting the fuel lines seemed so. . . permanent. While I didn't want to say it out loud, I felt very regretful doing such a thing, though it was already in complete disrepair, and it wasn't like I could leave in that thing alone. I would need some sort of other component. Like. . . a launch. A rocket launch that I attached to.

"It was a test launch," I announced loudly. "There was a major systems malfunction followed by a parachute failure. The trajectory—" Clint cut me off.

"Miscalculated?" He looked at me with a smile.

"Keep going, Jack. Ignore him." Annie gave him a look and then they both turned back to me.

"Yes, a miscalculation. The air was worse than we needed it to be. A high-pressure system had moved in abruptly below. I remember it being really stormy down here when I crashed," I said, thinking back as hard as I could. "I need to report this. They've probably already announced me as deceased." Annie's eyes got wide as she nodded.

"Okay, who do you need to call? Who is 'they'?" Annie didn't move or go for the rotary phone on the wall. They both just looked at me.

"I'm still not entirely sure. Perhaps I will know more later," I said in defeat.

"I know!" Clint hollered. "We need to call *Houston*."

"This is not *Apollo 13.*" Annie rolled her eyes. I couldn't stop thinking about the craft getting struck by lightning and destroying its surroundings.

"Clint is right," I said. Annie's eyes got wide.

"I am? I mean, yes; I am." Clint nodded, smiling.

"About the fuel lines. That thing is a ticking timebomb if more weather comes through. I'd hate to cause more strain to you than I already have." Annie shook her head as I spoke.

"You are no trouble at all. We haven't had this much fun in years. Have we, Clint?" She crossed her arms and waited for his reply.

"Remember when my cousin Bobby visited? I thought that was pretty fun. He brought the cannon, and we shot pumpkins up on that hill and—" Clint caught eyes with Annie. "Yeah, no, this really does top even the pumpkin palooza. We like having you here, Martian."

"We really do." Annie's voice was like hearing the song of an angel.

As Annie and Clint worked out the details of which method of transportation and when we would leave, I walked over to the front porch. The sun had risen to its full glory in the sky, and it was working overtime to dry out the ground. Spring in this region was known to be wet. I pondered why I knew that, considering that perhaps I lived nearby, when I thought back to my uniform. Could there be more information to be taken from it? Memories that could come back?

"Where did I put my suit?" Annie shuffled her feet.

"I am repairing it. I'm almost done," she said with uncertainty.

"Thank you. That is so kind of you." Annie was a very crafty woman. She cooked; she kept a ranch; she could sew stitches and my uniform. . . She was the most beautiful catch in the universe. "May I see it?" She nodded and went to retrieve it, returning a moment later. I recalled yesterday how it had been in tatters. Today, it looked like she must have worked through the night, as most of the holes had been sewn up. I flipped it to the back. A sharp object had torn through the top layer, and the suit's insulation had been sticking out of it, yet today, it was readable.

"*NebulaX.*" I read the company name aloud. "Can we call them?" Clint and Annie both nodded.

"Yes, of course. Are you feeling up to that?" I hadn't considered the question before now.

"I just can't shake this feeling like. . . I have somewhere I need to be. Urgently," I said, looking out the window, up at the sky.

"You need to be up there, but you're down here instead. I get it, Captain Floaty Pants." Clint put his arm around me like we were sharing a moment. Annie let out a sigh.

"Let me see what I can find out online. There's got to be a phone number somewhere," she said, pulling out a laptop computer from a desk drawer. As I looked to the sky, with Clint's arm still around me, I felt my emotions change.

"I'm sorry. That can wait," I said. Annie looked back at me, clearly confused.

"Are you sure? Why?"

"My mind says to call, but my heart says to wait. I'm feeling like I wouldn't be of much use while my memory is still mostly incomplete. I remember part of the crash, but that's it. I feel like a stranger in my own life."

"An alien on this ranch," Clint added, nodding.

"Okay, let's go, then," Annie announced. "Has everyone been fed?" she asked Clint.

"Now that you mention it, I'm still a little peckish, and I see you have a table full of food—" She swatted his hand away.

"This is for our guest. If you're hungry, you can go home," she laughed. "I meant the animals."

"Yep. Trevor helped me this morning. He had to come back home to get some clothes and to drop off your truck. He got his stick shift unstuck." He pulled out a set of keys from his pants pocket and handed them to Annie. "After the big rush to get out of here, he forgot to grab his backpack that had his change of clothes in it." Annie smiled.

"When do they get back? I can't wait to see that baby."

"Tomorrow. Just one more night in the hospital." *Hospital.* The word triggered another memory for me. I was in the hospital not that long ago. It felt recent, but also that so much time had passed by already. Yes, I was there; I could see my shoes on the white tile floor as I held my head in my hands. I wasn't the patient.

"Ready?" Annie asked, touching my arm ever so gently. Her fingers were cool to the touch. I swallowed the lump forming in my throat.

"Yes," I said, with a nod.

*****

I followed Annie and Clint to the horse corral. The horse I rode yesterday, Whisper, came running up to greet Annie.

"Hello, my pretty lady," she said and gave her an apple from her pocket.

"I hope you have treats to share," Clint said, pointing at his horse.

"Here's my proof, Jack: Clint, I have no more apples. What do you have?" Clint shuffled for a minute and pulled out a large swath of carrots from the vest he wore. "See? I knew it." Clint shrugged.

"Fine. But this doesn't change anything. They still love me for me." After all of the horses got carrots, and I fed them a few myself, Annie and Clint got to saddling.

"He can use your dad's saddle. I doubt he would mind," Clint said, grabbing a beautiful leather-tooled saddle from a stand in the barn next to the corral.

"Last time we talked, he told me that he can't see himself ever riding a horse again with his knee problems. So yeah, you're right." Annie wiped off her forehead. "Wow. Can someone turn off the heat?" The air to me felt quite cool. Perhaps sixty degrees. These Wyoming folk were just built differently.

"Okay, Cosmo. I need you to get on this horse so we can adjust the stirrups." Clint motioned for me to walk over. I tried to move as expertly as they did without bringing attention to my dizziness that still lingered. I put my left foot in the stirrup and grabbed the saddle horn and swung my right leg over.

"Great. It almost looks like you've done this before," Clint said, with a kindness to his voice. Today, the reins felt natural in my hands. Perhaps I had ridden in my lifetime other than yesterday? Clint quickly elongated the stirrups. "One more thing. It's pretty bright out here. You're gonna need a hat, and I ain't givin' you mine. So here, take this one." Clint handed me a well-loved western hat. I put it on, my eyes feeling relieved like someone pulled a shade in front of a bright window.

"Thank you. I needed that," I said, relishing in the sun protection. Annie and Clint were on their horses a moment later.

"How's the gravity over there, Major Tomfoolery?" Clint asked.

"Feels just fine, thanks," I said, grabbing hold of the reins.

"You're on Buckwheat. He's the largest horse we have and also the slowest. He's a 'stop and taste the grass' kind of guy, but don't worry, he will follow our horses. So, you can just sit back and enjoy the ride." Annie's words were reassuring until we started riding. The speed that Clint and Annie took off was intimidating. Buckwheat was slower, to my appreciation, but I still felt like we were in a fight to break the orbital velocity. Lucky for me, I was used to this feeling, and when I closed my eyes, it felt like I was back in flight.

"Here, Jack—go ahead of me. I'll follow you so Buckwheat doesn't go too fast," Annie said, holding back her smile.

"I feel good. This is. . . comfortable. I think I've ridden before," I said.

When we reached the craft, it was more tattered and shambled than I remembered. It was shaped like an upside-down basket, and everything except the middle had been flattened by design. On impact, the sides of it took all of the force so that the astronaut inside had a greater chance at survival. Now that I was seeing the wreckage with all five senses and a good night's sleep, I was questioning how I managed to survive in what was left of this. *God, I see that this was all You, and I thank You for sparing my life. You must not be done with me yet, and I pray that I can bring glory to You through the time I have left.*

"I don't know how you did it, Commander. This crash looks pretty bad." Clint dismounted from his horse, and Annie and I followed suit.

"And you know this because of your bathroom reading of 'Spaceship Weekly'?" Annie busted up laughing.

"No, Annie. I read 'Science Weekly' in the bathroom if you must know. And my dad was the sheriff, remember? I used to see some pretty bad plane wrecks where I grew up." He turned to me. "We had a landing strip about fifteen miles from here. A little bit of bad weather and some strong mountain winds—man, it looked about like this." I nodded.

"That sounds like what I went through." The memories flooded back. "But most of the problem for me was I didn't break the atmosphere when we launched." Clint nodded.

"You didn't get high enough, and the weather here sucked you in like Granny's vacuum cleaner after she hosted Saturday night cribbage. Someone could drop a diamond ring, but she wouldn't reach down to get it. In the vacuum it goes. Ain't nothin' spared that dropped on that floor."

"That's quite the comparison," Annie said, staring at Clint. "Anyway. . ." she trailed off.

"Actually, yes. It's just like that. I mean, except for the cribbage part," I said, smiling. Clint beamed with pride.

"See, Annie? I'm smarter than you thought."

"Smarter than you look in that chicken paisley shirt," she laughed again, and it was like the sound of angels singing. There was a glow to her skin this morning that I attributed to her olive skin tone. I thought she was tanning before my eyes.

"I got the clippers. Want to help me cut the lines, Sir Launch-a-lot?" Annie rolled her eyes and smirked.

"You just got an endless supply of these nicknames? Are you sure you aren't reading 'Science Weekly KIDS' instead?" She tapped her foot.

"That would explain the pictures and the games in the back." He put his hand up to his chin. "Anyway," he turned to me, "you find and I cut. How does that sound?" I nodded, though I felt unsure that I would know my way around the craft. I may have flown the thing, but did I understand the engineering of it? I surely hoped so.

Instinctively, I walked over to an outside panel. "Annie, do you still have that—" she cut me off.

"Here ya go," handing me the multi-tool. I found a flathead screwdriver.

"Thank you." I looked over at her, catching her eyes and for a moment, it was like looking directly into the sun. We aren't supposed to do it. It burns the retinas. But sometimes, it happens by accident.

"Earth to Jack." Clint waved his hand in front of my face.

"Wow, you know his name!" Annie crossed her arms and cocked her eyebrow.

"Sure, I do. You're giving me a complex by using the nicknames, is all. You know, nicknames are a form of building a brotherhood. They are *friendly.* Look it up."

"Is it, uh, always like this?" I motioned to them, wondering the dynamic of their constant bickering, but admittedly, I found it highly entertaining.

"Oh. . . Yeah, it is. Our parents were best friends back in the day, and we were born around the same time. Clint's first word was 'Annie' and mine was 'eww.' It's in our nature to bicker, but we're just the oldest pals." She crossed her arm and he nodded. "I even introduced him to his wife, though I never thought he could pull it off."

"Alright, alright. Let the man work, Annie. I'm burning up out here," Clint said, to which Annie agreed.

Once I removed the panel, I slowly lifted it over my head and threw it off to the side. My strength was coming back to me, and only my wounds remained as the reminder of the crash. Now, I was just waiting for my memory to return.

Inside the panel were all sorts of wires and tubes. "Here's the fuel lines," I pointed, to which Clint immediately cut without further question. Annie, however, had one.

"Are you sure?" she asked, after they were already cut.

"They say fuel on them," I said, laughing. In the tiniest little letters, FUEL was in a white font. But I didn't need to read that to know. "I just knew. I remember this." As I looked at the inner parts of the mechanical side of the spacecraft, my hands moved with their own memories. I pulled a connector out of a port. I instructed Clint to cut another wire that was the power reserve to the entire craft. I even unscrewed a plate on the underbelly of the wires.

"What's that?" Annie asked.

"I think it's the black box equivalent. Better take that with me."

CHAPTER 5: ANNIE

THE GRAVITY BETWEEN US

I wanted to tell Jack. Every cell in my body wanted to tell Jack the rest of what he said while he was dreaming. That his brother, Hank, may be or have been in some dire straits. Keeping this from him felt wrong, but I also hadn't felt the Holy Spirit urge me to do so yet, either.

This morning was kind of a "rip the tape off" moment—I thought, here we go. I'll just tell him and let the chips fall where they may. But Clint interrupted and the relief I felt was palpable. I didn't think this was my secret to tell and besides, his memory was trickling back slowly. It was probably only a matter of time before he remembered what happened. Then, if he wished, he could tell *me* about it.

Riding back to the crash site, I could barely take my eyes off of Jack while he rode the horse. He looked like a natural. It didn't hurt that he was dressed the part, too. Clint gave him an old hat to wear and by golly when that space man put it on, I felt my heart drop into my stomach. He may have had amnesia, but this man was a cowboy, and he didn't even know it.

Then he dropped the bombshell that even though Buckwheat was ridin' like crazy on him, he was comfortable. And that he *thought* he'd ridden before. Yes, sir, you had ridden before, because there wasn't a single city slicker in the world who could just jump on Buckwheat and ride that naturally.

When we reached the crash, Clint and Jack got to work. Today, seeing Jack in his element, cutting lines and pulling cords, I saw a glimpse of who he was shining through his amnesia. He might have been a natural cowboy, but he was a really smart guy, too. Like, engineer type mind. I could have used someone like him to look at our electric fences that hadn't worked right since they had been installed in the late '90's.

Then he pulled that small metal plate off. I wanted to see it for myself—to find out its significance in order to help his memory along. But I held back.

Clint pulled two shovels off of his horse and handed one to Jack. "We just need to dig a fire line around your spaceship in a circle. Like this," he said, showing Jack how it could be done. Jack nodded and with both men working hard, it was done in a few minutes. "There. Now, if it does catch fire, considering there was some fuel leaking, it has dirt to meet. If it crosses this line, that would be one heck of a fire." Jack wiped sweat from his brow, though the work looked effortless for him.

Thunder clapped in the distance. "Uh oh," I said, looking up at the darkening sky. "It's coming for us. We better hurry." I zipped up my coat in preparation for the downpour that could have happened at any time.

"I'm almost ready," Jack said, as he went to the other side of the craft, where I took the panel off to free him. "I just need to take one last look inside." He disappeared for a moment and reemerged with a backpack. "Okay, we're done here." Small rain drops started to sprinkle on our heads lightly.

"I'm going to hurry back. I think I left my windows open, and Jaylee is at the grocery store. If I ruin any more of that carpet. . ." he trailed off, as he swiftly got into the saddle. "Take it easy, Space Cowboy."

"You'll be forced to replace it with the wood floors she's been wanting since you married her?" I crossed my arms, trying to hide the fact that I was pleased he was leaving. The hard parts were done. My mind wanted to know the contents of Jack's backpack he pulled from the craft. I hoped that maybe now that we were alone, he would tell me.

"We better get back, too. This levee on this rain cloud is about to burst," I said, not liking the looks of the thunderhead above us. Jack nodded, and we both got back into the saddles; his movement was effortless once again.

A loud crack of thunder came in right over our heads; I ducked instinctively. "We should take shelter. I don't want anything to happen out here." Looking over at Jack, he was staring up at the rapidly darkening sky.

"How about right there?" He pointed to the largest juniper tree the ranch had. Last year, a branch was cut down just out of curiosity and the rings on it counted well over five hundred years. I nodded in agreement.

"We better hurry," I said, giving Whisper a nudge to gallop faster. Once we both reached the tree, I swiftly dismounted and stood under its large, shadowy branches. Jack crouched down beside me, and we each held on to our horses' lead ropes as they stood beside each other.

"Will the horses get struck?" he asked, and I shrugged my shoulders.

"While it's true that horses attract lightning, I think that's more when they are out riding. Something with the friction of their horseshoes running on land. They will want shelter just as much as we do but for now, I'm praying they will be okay." The horses instinctively walked a few feet to the other side of the juniper tree where the branches were higher and stood underneath.

"We should pray together," Jack said, already closing his eyes. And we did pray. A few words out loud, a few to ourselves. After a few minutes, the clouds unleashed a heavy rain pour, and it wasn't long before my teeth were chattering.

"Here," he said, moving a little closer to me as he held his arm out. "I didn't survive a crash just to watch a beautiful woman freeze to death." If I had any warmth left in my body, it went straight to my cheeks when he called me beautiful. As he wrapped his arm around my shoulders and pulled me sideways towards him in an embrace, I felt his strength. His arms were muscular and toned. I felt safe in his grasp and like I'd finally found my way home after years of looking. I hoped the rain would never end.

Lightning struck within yards of us, and I let out a shriek. It frightened me to see it that close by, but the rain pouring off the juniper let out an intoxicating scent that was only the result of a Wyoming storm. In this dry climate, when it finally does rain, if you could bottle the scent, it would be sold all over the world. It smells like sagebrush, a woodsy forest, and the purest moisture, straight from heaven. The scent can bring out wild emotions in people—it's like our natural instincts take over when given that big of a dose of nature. That must be why it doesn't rain very much here. People can't handle it.

Jack's grip on my shoulder tightened when I was frightened by the lightning. "Don't worry; we're safe here," he said under his breath. Judging by his tone, I knew the lightning wasn't the only thing feeling supercharged. This romantic tension was having an effect on him, too.

I turned to him; I couldn't help myself. At first, he looked away for about a moment, but his face came back to me fast. We were only a few inches away from our lips touching. He smelled like the wilds of this tree. I closed my eyes, wanting to feel his lips rather than see them; I wanted to experience what a kiss with this man was like by touch alone. Whisper let out a loud neigh that startled me. I pretended it didn't happen by staying still, but I felt a pause. I waited for him to move closer to my lips, but he didn't move. I opened my eyes back up, and he was pulling back.

"I'm sorry," he said, putting his head in his free hand. "I just can't do this until I know who I am." I nodded, feeling disappointment, despite my understanding, and a little embarrassment. I was trying not to react emotionally when he continued. "I want to... It's just that... What if it changes things when I remember? What if. . ." he trailed off. I knew the "what ifs" were great. He could have been a married astronaut who lost his ring. He might have had a wife *and* children. He could have been in charge of a religious following where everyone had three wives. It was a chance that we shouldn't have taken, and finally, I relented.

"You're totally right, Jack. And I'm sorry. I don't need to be some temptress out here in the wilderness, cozying up to you under a tree in a rainstorm." I smiled, trying to lighten the mood.

"A very *romantic* rainstorm," he winked. The rain was slowing as the clouds moved on. The sky was starting to lighten. "I think it's passed," he said, but he didn't move his arm. I got the feeling he didn't want to hurt my feelings, so I crawled out from under the tree, thinking the cold rain could do me some good.

We got back on our horses without a word and started to ride while I prayed about my feelings.

Lord, I know this man literally just fell out of the sky yesterday, but I have never felt more drawn to a person in my entire life. He makes my heart skip like a spooked colt. If this ain't right, Lord, please rein me in.

"The crash," Jack said, with a low tone. I was just thankful the subject had changed from our near kiss. I needed something else to distract me and keep my thoughts clean.

"Yeah? What about it?" I asked.

"I think there were corners cut," he trailed off. My heart sank. *Lord, please be near this man in his memory loss.*

I could have pressed him with questions. I had plenty— what did he remember? Was there something in particular that stood out? But instead, I let him think. This situation was larger than me. Larger than my ranch. It was maybe the biggest hurdle I'd seen someone experience in my lifetime, but it wasn't too big for God. In fact, I saw God working through him almost immediately after I thought that, as Jack looked over at me and smiled.

"What are you smilin' about, Orbit Outlaw?"

"Not you with the nicknames," he shook his head and laughed, giving a shrug. "You have chickens," he grinned, seeing a coop not too far off. We were almost back to the corral where we started.

"And the astronaut likes chickens?" I was totally confused.

"Look how funny they are. Oh, my. Are they *fighting?*" His voice went from humor to shock in a matter of seconds. I peered off and noticed a scuffle of feathers and could hear the squawks.

"Umm. . . I think they are, yes. Oh, my word. Someone must have mixed up the flock. Clint." I rolled my eyes, reaching for my radio, but it appeared I had forgotten it again like most days. "We're almost there." I picked up the pace on Whisper, reaching the coop. The birds started to scatter as we both got off our horses. I handed Jack Whisper's lead rope. Do you want to take them to the corral? I can handle this," I said, grudgingly. The birds were still trying to fight, even after I showed up.

"Are you sure? Why are they acting like that?" I stepped into the coop area, plucking a bird up with my bare hands.

"Because this one is new, and the others are trying to establish their pecking order. The bully doesn't want to lose her place in the world just because someone bigger than her has been introduced." Just then, Clint was seen riding in from his cabin a hundred yards away.

"There you are," he said, sheepishly. "What took you so long to get back?" I tried to think of anything else so my cheeks wouldn't redden and make me look like we had been up to something. Though I wouldn't call that nothing, Clint didn't need to know the details.

"We got caught in the storm," Jack said, saving me from an awkward explanation. I thanked him with my eyes. Clint didn't miss a beat.

"Yeah, I bet you did." He got off his horse and the three of us stood there like three points to a triangle. I looked at Clint and Jack, thinking back to the pecking order around the ranch and smiled.

"Anyway," I said, changing the subject. "Jack was just about to take the horses back to the corral. Can you show him where we put the saddles? Also, where did this bird come from? She's been treated pretty *fowl,* if you ask me." Clint laughed dramatically at my joke.

"Good one, Annie. Real clever," he said.

"I try," I shrugged. "But really. Don't distract me with flattery. She's new, Clint. Explain." I cocked my brow at him.

"Well, the Michael's farm next door had too many and…" he trailed off.

"Alright. Well, she's a little roughed up but hopefully, that was the end of it. She's actually quite pretty. I don't think we've ever had a Lavender hen before," I said, smiling. Clint knew that I was going to love this bird.

"Jaylee said that you've always wanted one," he said.

"Ah, and speaking of your better half," I said, "what time is dinner tonight?"

"Want to meet around six? She went to get some supplies for the smoker. I thought we could do the steaks in it."

"You are just looking for an excuse to use your new birthday present and in this case, it's benefiting me, so happy birthday to you," I said with a laugh.

"It's your birthday?" Jack asked Clint.

"A few days ago. The misses got me the smoker, so this will be her maiden voyage tonight." Jack looked pained. I wondered what he was thinking—if he was considering his own birthday or something else. I was going to pull him aside and ask how he was doing, but Clint patted him on the back. "Alright, Comet Kid. Let's get these horses in the corral, and I'll even show you the best way to shovel up manure."

"Gee, thanks. I can't wait," Jack said dryly. But there was a skip to his step as the men walked the horses back.

They spent the rest of the afternoon working on the ranch. After the horses were put back, the manure was shoveled, and Jack still had gas left in his tank, Clint took him over to the sheep pasture, which was out of sight. I only knew because Jaylee came and knocked on my front door while I was cleaning up my kitchen. I didn't normally do housework in the middle of the day, but with everyone coming over tonight, I wanted to take some time and make it presentable.

"Hey, girlie," Jaylee said, letting herself in after a swift knock. Her tumbling, thick, red hair always reminded me of Rapunzel. She was a striking beauty, with dark green eyes and fair skin. Clint roped in a serious prize with her. She was also very caring but had a touch of gossipy nature about her. I always prayed that I would guard my mouth and heart when I was around her. I didn't want to partake in gossip, but as everyone knows, it's extremely hard to resist when it's presented to you.

"Hi, friend. I'm just getting ready for tonight," I said, as I scrubbed down my sink. Jaylee let out a laugh.

"I can see that," she said, looking me up and down. I was wearing a fresh set of clothes—a feminine blouse, sparkle jeans, and a pink floral apron that belonged to my mother.

"Oh, well, we got caught in the rain, and I had to change," I said, shrugging my shoulders.

"That rain will make you do some crazy things. . . That's how Clint got me to agree to marry him, you know. Pulled over in a rainstorm and asked me to get out where we danced, and he got down on one knee. I blame the smell of the storm. It was like I was in a Nicholas Spark's movie. . ." she smiled, as she shared the memory. Though Clint and I teased each other relentlessly, he was like a brother to me, and Jaylee was now like a sister. I cared for these people with the fiercest love of God that I could.

"Girl. . . It nearly got me out there. I have been feeling some things for him. . ." I stopped short. I got caught up in the conversation. I looked back at Jaylee, her eyes widening. Like I thought before, I loved Jaylee. Very, very much. But anything I told her could and would be used against me by Clint or anyone else that she came in contact with, because the woman must have had the rest of Big Horn, Wyoming on a group text, and she would be sharing this information immediately.

"Oh really? So, you like him then?" Jaylee pulled a barstool out from under the kitchen island, getting herself comfortable for the information coming her way. As she reached for her phone, no doubt to take notes or record the audio, I paused.

"I'm not sure yet. But I'd like to just keep this between us until I know." Jaylee looked extremely disappointed, but I didn't care. I meant, I did care—again, so much love here—but this situation was bigger than me. Jack was involved. And his reputation. Imagine how I would look if it turned out he was married? Or, in a relationship? The already depressing and thin bi-weekly newspaper would have a great front page: 'Lonely Annie falls for married Space Jockey!" It was a risk I wasn't willing to take. *Lord, please guard my mouth and do not let me give in to the folly of gossip.*

Jaylee pulled out her phone and looked down at it; her fingers contemplating opening her messages. I turned back to cleaning the sink. I asked her not to speak about it, and I had to trust that she would honor that. A moment later when I turned back around to grab my drying towel off the kitchen island, her phone was put away.

"So, Clint is pretty excited to use the smoker," I said, nonchalantly. Really just to change the subject as this topic was the last thing I wanted to talk about and by the look on Jaylee's face, she agreed.

"Yep. I got all the stuff to go with it right here," she said, remembering why she came by in the first place. "I thought I could pop this casserole dish in your oven an hour before we eat, so it's ready by dinner? Scalloped potatoes." I nodded.

"Of course. I was thinking of making dessert. Remember that pie that my mom used to make at every turn of the seasons?" Jaylee closed her eyes and smiled.

"Apple strawberry blueberry fiasco pie." We both let out a giggle. "She made that for our engagement party, too." I thought back to the reception they held at the local church. Seemed like forever ago that my parents were here, but it had barely been a year. I didn't realize it until now, but I was longing for a visit with them. Something face to face; phone calls were not going to cut it forever.

"I think I'm going to make it," I said, walking to my fridge to see what produce I had.

"You sure? Do you want some help?" The running joke around the ranch was that I didn't know how to cook. It wasn't entirely true; I cooked things all the time that I thought were delicious and edible and for the record, a future husband would enjoy. For instance, I could grill a steak like there was no tomorrow. I'd perfected a tater tot casserole. I could simmer a chili in the slow cooker all day long and have crumbly, honey cornbread baked to perfection. What I struggled with was this pie. I tried to make it once before, at a holiday gathering, and it went horribly wrong. Sure, that was *eons* ago—at least ten years. But this was where all of the teasing and the jokes stemmed from: This one, hilariously bad pie where I mistakenly mixed up the salt and the sugar. In my defense, they were in very similar looking Mason jars in the cupboard.

"No, I think I'll manage. Thank you, though." Jaylee nodded and didn't try to hide the look of concern from her expression.

"I better run back home. You're all dressed up, and I feel like a slob in comparison." Jaylee was wearing a baggy sweater and loose-fitting jeans, but it was what I was used to seeing her in, so I didn't really notice.

"Don't go gettin' fancy on my accord. This is the only top I had that doesn't have a faint smell of hay or horses on it." I pointed to my slinky, ¾ sleeve top that had pink paisley with pops of blue that matched my eyes. While it was true it was the freshest clothing I owned, it also made my eyes pop, and I just wanted to feel beautiful for a change. Jaylee nodded and left, while I got started on the pie.

The recipe was simple enough; you just blend your fruits together in a brown sugar-y mixture and bake in a buttery flakey crust. I found a handwritten recipe card from my mother and started in on the crust.

CHAPTER 6: JACK

SADDLE UP, SPACEMAN

At first, I thought Clint was trying to test me. What started with corralling the horses turned into lifting hay bales to reorganize the barn.

"We need to get all of this hay that's down here on the ground, where it's easy to retrieve, up there in that loft." I followed his gaze as he stood with his hands on his waist and looked up.

"Why would we do such a thing? Don't you need it on the ground?" Clint thought about my question for a minute and then answered.

"We can get to it easily, but so can the other critters that like to pass through here. We need it to be up there where it's much, much harder to get to for the deer, rabbits, cows, whatever might accidentally wander in here and decide they are going to feast on our alfalfa."

"You're telling me that you have wild cows roaming the ranches and are at risk of one of them discovering how to open a somewhat complicated lever on the barn door—one that requires two hands and poseable thumbs—and then proceeding to eat everything inside?" I cocked an eyebrow.

"You summed it up better than I ever could have." He patted me on the back, and we moved a few hay bales up to the loft using a rickety wooden ladder before I had a better idea.

"Do you have a rope?" Clint nodded.

"I got more rope than they have in stock at the hardware store. Why, what are you thinking?" A half an hour later, we had an elaborate pulley system and effortlessly moved hundreds of pounds of hay up while staying firmly planted on the dirt. "It works, Star Man. You some kind of engineer or somethin'?"

"Something like that," I said, smiling. Things were hazy, but this sort of work did seem natural to me.

"Well, you're a natural for ranch work, I'll give ya that," he grinned. After we moved up a dozen bales, Clint decided it was enough to have a reserve in case the animals did grow poseable thumbs and turned into *MacGyver* proteges. "Now, when we need those bales, we just use your best friend to get them down!”

“My best friend?” I gave him a puzzled look. Clint ran back up the ladder and kicked one off the loft.

“Gravity!” I let out a low laugh.

“Was that your first time using that word in a sentence?”

“Har har. I’ll have you know that I looked at the science magazines, and they are *not* for children. They are for *young adults,* like myself.”

“Isn’t the term ‘young adult’ for like 13–18?” I crossed my arms but couldn’t contain my laughter.

“Whatever. It’s still good readin’. Maybe I’ll drop one off to you. I think I just got one in the mail. It hasn’t been with me in the bathroom yet,” Clint said, matter-of-factly.

“That’s so. . . Generous of you, Clint.” He nodded, smiling.

After the hay bale move, we went back outside where the weather had heated up tremendously. Beads of sweat covered my forehead under my cowboy hat.

“What is it. . . one hundred degrees out here?” Clint shook his head.

"Sixty-one degrees. It feels pretty hot up here though, don't it? It's because we're at such a high elevation with no cloud cover. We're just closer to the sunup here, I guess. You know, last year at this time, we had three feet of snow on the ground. Boy, you chose the right year to crash land on this ranch!" I nodded, picking up my backpack that I had set outside the barn and pulling out a hydration multiplier that was sticking out of the front pocket. *I know what this is,* I thought, as I downed the gummy gel, feeling a jolt of sugary energy from it. "By the way, what's in that thing? An extra pair of drawers?" He gave me a cockeyed look and pointed to the backpack.

"Well, if you must know, yes, I saw some of those in there. But it also appears to have some of my other clothes and personal items. Whatever I already had in here, I didn't look that closely." I was dying to go through it and see what memories came trickling back to me, but Clint had another project for us, so this was going to have to wait.

"Good. Now, along with Annie's dad's hand-me-downs, you'll have a real set of clothes. If you ever want to borrow one of my nice shirts. . ." He pointed to his chicken paisley get up and looked at me expectantly.

"Oh," I said. Knowing how much Annie made fun of his clothes, I wasn't sure I wanted to be associated with such items. "You are so kind, *buddy.*" That did the trick; Clint was beaming ear to ear.

"Okay, we better get back to the chores. Man, I was totally joshin' you on the hay; I wanted to see if you had it in you. Later, we better go in and kick all of that off the loft because Annie likes to hang out up there sometimes. There's a roof hatch that opens, and she's got a telescope up there." Clint spun around on his heels while I relished in the fact that she enjoyed star gazing. "Now, next is a task that we actually need to do: I have some tractor tires that I can't let get cracked out in the sun. Now that it's warming up, I need to flip them and hose them down with a UV protectant."

"Got any that's safe for skin? I'm baking over here." I felt my skin starting to redden in the warming, spring weather. Something told me the only daylight I'd gotten recently had been from inside a simulator.

After we flipped the tires and ensured that they wouldn't be destroyed in the coming weeks, I wondered how long my time on this ranch would be. It seemed frightful to think that by the time this task would have needed to be done again, I would have still been here, gripping my hands together in prayer for my memory. *God, please deliver me from this amnesia before too long!* As I prayed, I was reminded that no matter what happened, God works for the good of all things, and His plan is greater than anything I could have wanted for myself. *I just prayed that my season of waiting wasn't more than I could handle.*

As I started to look around me for any sort of sign or remembrance of my identity, I started to see how Clint reminded me of my brother, Hank, although I couldn't quite pinpoint why. Perhaps everything reminded me of him because I wanted to remember. My heart longed to speak with him. But as the day went on, that empty longing was replaced by a joyful heart from spending time with these great people. Annie was the most beautiful woman I'd ever seen —possibly the only thing I knew for certain—and Clint's fellowship was as enjoyable to be around as humorous.

Once we were done with the sheep turning and ensured their prized wool wouldn't be awkwardly bleached in the wrong spots, the last task that I was *sure* was more of a ruse than a necessity, Clint was pleased with the day.

"Let's call it," he said, looking at his leather wristwatch. "I gotta turn on the smoker and figure out how it works before supper tonight, or my wife is going to return it," he said with a wide-eyed look.

"I can't wait to meet her," I said with a laugh under my breath. "She sounds like a real no-nonsense woman."

"Speaking of women," Clint said, stepping closer towards me as we walked back to the base of the ranch where the housing was, "what are your intentions with Annie?" His tone wasn't exactly serious, nor was it lighthearted. I shrugged. "I've seen the chemistry between you. If Einstein was here, he would try to bottle it up as palpable matter."

"She's. . . absolutely beautiful. I'm floored looking at her. But I also don't know if I am single and just thinking these thoughts while I have lost part of my identity makes me feel slimy." I slumped my shoulders. *Lord, I feel in my heart that I am single and ready to mingle. But I want to know for sure before acting on anything. Please help me keep that virtue.*

"I respect that," Clint said, nodding. He was looking forward, not making eye contact with me as we walked. "If you are single, I think you two would make a good match." Hearing his blessing of the relationship was an extension of kindness.

"Thanks, man. I appreciate that. I just worry about who I am. What if I'm some sort of jerk that she wouldn't like?" Clint shook his head.

"I'm not fully brushed up on amnesia and how that works. But, from what I've seen played out on soap operas that my wife watches, I think who you are now is a good indication of who you are in real life." His words were reassuring. "If you wanted to know for sure, I might have a way to look into things," Clint said, pulling out his phone. "We could image search the web for you and see what we find. An astronaut such as yourself must have something out there, right?" The idea wasn't terrible, but I admitted I was fearful of what I might have found out.

"Okay, let's do it. Do you have a signal?" I looked around us. We were almost to Annie's farmhouse and still several hundred yards from his house.

"I will be in Wi-Fi range in about ten more feet," he said, rushing to take a few big steps. "Okay, now let's get a photo." I took off my borrowed cowboy hat and turned so the sun wasn't directly in my eyes. Clint leaned back and snapped a picture.

"Now what?" I asked.

"We just upload it into this search engine here. . . and, voila. It's thinking." The nerves at this moment were crippling me. My hands, already hot from the work we'd been doing, were sweating uncontrollably. My knees felt weak. It was like yesterday all over again except yesterday, I didn't feel fear. I just felt unsettled.

"Well? Anything?" Clint had gone silent while he was looking at the results.

"Nice to meet you, Jack Carter."

*****

Back in my temporary cabin, I thought about the results from Clint's internet search. There wasn't much about me, just an article about the new technology that was being utilized at NebulaX, where I was an engineer and now, astronaut. Well, where I wanted to be, anyway. This was my first launch, and according to the world wide web, I had yet to break the atmosphere.

I wanted there to be more about me. I wanted to see a Wikipedia with my entire life laid out—professional achievements and most importantly, *personal.* Sigh. I prayed to God, asking him for any other morsel of my identity He was willing to share, knowing full and well His timeline is different from mine, and waited. I said my name a hundred or so times to see if anything would come back, and I did some conversational drills. "Hi, I'm Jack Carter. That's me, Jack Carter." Nothing.

Then, I remembered my backpack. I couldn't believe how quickly I had cast that aside when I returned to my living quarters! Carefully picking it back up, I sat it atop the old desk as if it held the secrets of the universe. For me, it very well could have. I unzipped it slowly, feeling the metal teeth of the zipper widen. Then, I folded it open. Inside was some much-needed clothing, and I set that aside. Next, I found a bar of chocolate. It looked fancy—perhaps it was something familiar? The package was beautiful. The label read, "Moonstruck Chocolate" and was a special variety. A clue? I set the bar aside and kept looking. A few dehydrated food rations were scattered along the bottom and a pack of beef jerky read, "Made In Wyoming" along the top in prominent letters. Where in the world could I have gotten this? But after the jerky, I was looking at the bottom in defeat.

"Lord, please help me!" I called out, frantically searching through the bag with nothing known about me but my name and that I had people. A family. A brother whom I loved deeply and who was very, very sick. If not already gone. "Lord, please tell me if he is gone." I felt emotion overtake me. My body shook. This felt very foreign to me, but I didn't cry. My body wouldn't make the tears. I sat down at the desk and the rickety chair groaned as if it was letting out its last breath. I laid the backpack flat in front of me, and when I did, I saw an outline of something in the front pocket. When I slowly pulled back the zipper that was holding it in place, my fingers reached in to feel the outline of a book. I closed my eyes, pulling it out. When I had the book in my hands in front of my face, I opened it. It was a traveler's copy of the Holy Bible. I laughed.

"God, you sure do have a sense of humor," I said aloud, realizing here I was in full despair over my lost identity and all I had on me was a bar of chocolate, some spare clothes, and a Bible, telling me that whoever I was, I was made anew so that I could lean into Christ and His promises to get me through this crisis. I set the Bible down and prayed.

*****

The sky told me that the time was nearing five in the evening. With no running water in this shack, I gathered my clothing and put it back in the backpack and went to Annie's to see about a shower. When I arrived, she was in a deep conversation with Clint and a redhead woman I'd yet to meet. I hesitated before walking in, as even through the screen door they were too immersed to notice me yet, and besides, I already knew that I was the topic of conversation. But I decided I didn't need to hear what they were saying, because they'd shown me nothing but the fact that they were good people, and I got the feeling that I didn't like to eavesdrop. I quickly knocked on the door.

"Come on in, Jack," Annie said, standing up from the kitchen table, lights up. I nodded, entering the home and immediately smelling some very comforting foods. My stomach grumbled; the breakfast feast Annie had prepared had worn off, and I was ready for more. I turned as the redheaded woman got up and stuck her hand out to shake mine.

"Jaylee. Nice to meet you, Jack." She had a warmth to her smile that seemed very eager to get to know me and all of my secrets.

"Pleasure to meet Clint's better half." I looked over at him while I shook her hand and smiled.

"You got that right," Clint said, holding up his glass of water as if he was looking for someone to say "cheers" with. I turned back to Annie.

"I was hoping that I could...uh, shower again. If it's not too much trouble." She smiled and nodded.

"The guest bath is all ready for you—I just put a towel and soap in there and some fresh clothes." I gripped the strap on my backpack that was slung over my shoulder.

"Thank you so much. I really appreciate it," I said, as we stared into each other's eyes. Though it was time to walk away, I couldn't break the gaze as her blue eyes twinkled back at me. She was looking at me expectantly, like she wanted me to tell her something, but I didn't know what. Clint cleared his throat, and she broke her gaze first. Had she not, I would still be searching her eyes for the roadmap to my life for the rest of the evening. "I'll be right out," I said finally, and she nodded.

Once I was cleared of the day's sweat and dirt, it felt amazing to change into my clean socks, boxers, and an undershirt. The air was chilly enough to warrant it, and it just felt great. Annie had laid out a pair of jeans and another button up shirt on the counter. There was also a laundry hamper that I put my dirty clothes into. When I emerged from the guest bathroom, I felt like a new man.

"Save some women for the rest of us, space cadet." Clint got up and whispered to me, as both women looked over to me with big smiles. I laughed in response, and Jaylee quickly looked away and playfully punched her husband in the arm. He pretended to be hurt, and then they shared a kiss.

CHAPTER 7: ANNIE
ZERO GRAVITY, ZERO CHILL

When Clint walked into my house this afternoon, he looked like he had something very important to announce. With all of our years of friendship, I'd never quite seen this look on his face.

"Cat got your tongue?" I said, as both Jaylee and I were staring at him. As I waited for him to walk in and sit down, I couldn't decide if he looked angry, upset, concerned, or like he had just gotten a whiff of the pie in the oven, which knowing his aversion to my baking, could have been all of the above.

"It's Jack," he grumbled, pulling out a chair at the table. My eyes widened, standing up.

"Is he okay?" I demanded.

"Yes, he's fine. He's in the cabin taking a minute."

"Taking a minute for what, Clint?" Jaylee pressed hard, so I didn't have to. I thanked her with my eyes.

"We did an image search of his face," Clint said, pulling his phone out of his pocket. "Here, look." He slid the phone to me across the table. Jaylee looked like she wanted to see it before anyone else, but she knew better than that. I picked it up. My hands felt like they were trembling as I mentally prepared to see a photo of him and his wife. Maybe his whole brood of beautiful, green-eyed children.

"There's nothing here," I said, releasing my breath. "Just his. . . name?" There was just a photo of him on the NebulaX website under the "Our Astronauts" tab. It was so simple and yet. . . I couldn't believe I hadn't thought to look at the website earlier. But other than his unbelievably handsome photo, where he was revealing a little of his confident smile that was making me melt just looking at it, I didn't understand. What had Clint's drawers in a bunch?

"His name, if you search it separately. . . He's single, Annie. And I am not about to be here when your father hears that you've run off with an astro-nut." Clint burst out in laughter. Jaylee rolled her eyes, and I just stood there, waiting for more information.

"What do you mean, he's single? Where did you surmise that information? From a company headshot that doesn't bother for a biography? I see nothing that touches on it. 'Here's Jack Carter. Astronaut. Seeks a blonde-haired, blue-eyed woman to call his own.' Show me." My tone was sarcastic but firm. Clint nodded, taking the phone back and then tapped on a social media icon.

"Here—click on the search bar. Type in his name. His profile is private but wham—relationship status: *single*." Clint looked all too proud of himself as I looked at the nearly empty profile. I stared at the photo, which was a faraway picture of a telescope. There was no hometown listed, no current city. No other information. Just a telescope and a 'single' status.

"It might not be him, Clint. I don't think that 'Jack Carter' is that uncommon of a name. I can think of lots of men named Jack that I've heard of," I said, sliding the phone back once again, but Jaylee snatched it up.

"It's like the name of an astronaut in a movie. Jack Carter? A little *too* fitting for this if you ask me," Jaylee said.

"You think this is all a set up?" Clint lowered his voice, playing into Jaylee's idea. "That maybe. . . he's a plant? Maybe. . . they've tapped this place with a bug and are listening to our every word?" He looked both ways over his shoulders for dramatic effect.

"No, babe. Not like that, but now that you say it, I don't know. What do we really know about this guy?" she whispered, not wanting to be heard by the hypothetical microphone strapped under the dining room table.

"Okay, guys. Enough. We don't know anything about him, other than his character, which is perfect." I crossed my arms. Both of them looked at me with a cock-eyed expression. Wrong choice of words. "I mean, he seems great. And that's the whole point. We don't know, he doesn't know... Let's just let him figure that out." I sighed, as we sat in deep conversation. We barely even heard the handsome astronaut knock on the door.

"Come on in, Jack," I said. My words felt like they were stuck in my throat. I hoped that he hadn't been standing there long but decided if he had heard my words about him being perfect, I wouldn't have denied it. I didn't regret saying it, and I tried to live in a way that if I said something about someone, I would have said it to their face if given the chance. This was no different here.

I watched as Jack met Jaylee. I could tell she was mildly flirty with him, but it didn't bother me. She was like that sometimes, even though she was married to Clint. Like she was always exploring if she made the right choice by marrying such a goofball. But I knew deep down that they had a true love. I just thought that Jaylee didn't have a close relationship with God and hadn't felt conviction for her flirtatious, gossipy ways. Though it was hard at times—quite often, actually—I was going to continue to do my best to love her despite it and pray that she found the conviction in her heart.

Now, standing face to face with the handsome astronaut, he asked about a shower. The tension between us was unbelievable. Since our near kiss this afternoon, my body had felt like it had a magnet only for him. I told him that he could shower in the guest bathroom, but he didn't walk away. Not yet. I knew he felt it too. All of me was drawn to all of him. All of this talk of who Jack was? I couldn't say it aloud, lest my friends would have thought I'd lost the plot. But the truth? I didn't even care who he was and while that scared me in a way, it also made me feel alive. Jack Carter was the most drop-dead handsome man I'd ever seen, but the magnetic attraction I felt to him transcended beauty and logic.

After I processed that thought, Clint made some annoying noise, and I finally got the strength to break my gaze with Jack. *God, help me fight these feelings if they aren't from You.* When he walked away, finally, I felt like my mind was sobering up. His gaze almost had me feeling like I was under a spell. Clint and Jaylee looked over at me, with wide eyes, then looked away in opposite directions pretending they didn't see it.

I went to the oven and prodded my pie for several minutes, unnecessarily. I checked the side dishes in the fridge. Checked my ice trays to make sure I still had a year's supply of ice, just in case any of my guests requested it in their water. As I was about to check the tightness of the pipe underneath the kitchen sink, Jaylee chimed in, breaking me out of my flurry of avoidance.

"If I didn't see it with my own eyes, I wouldn't have believed Clint when he told me, Annie," Jaylee spoke softly.

"Told you what?" I asked, looking away. I didn't want to see them right now while I was reflecting on the experience I had just had with Jack. Our connection felt predestined. Divine. *Otherworldly.*

"Clint said that you and Jack were soulmates," Jaylee said. I shot a look at them, expecting there to be laughter among them with such a statement.

"Soulmates? He's been here for 36 hours," I scoffed, praying to God at that very moment that this preposterous accusation would come true. How Clint picked up on that was beyond me, but there was nothing more in life than for that to be my fate.

"There's some things in life we just know, Annie," Clint said as he stood up, adjusting the waistline of his pants. "Well, I better check on the smoker," he said, as the guest bathroom door opened and Jack walked out. We all instinctively froze; even Clint stood there. Jaylee and I stared at him like he was the last man on earth, and we needed the garbage taken out. Jack walked over to him and Clint whispered something to him, and both men chuckled.

"C'mon, Jack. Let's go check the steaks," Clint said, putting his arm around Jack as they walked outside.

"You really think you see something between us?" I whispered to Jaylee. I didn't always trust her judgment, but I still was a glutton for punishment.

"A blind dog could see there is something happening here, Annie," Jaylee snorted as she talked.

"But is it from the Lord?" I asked rhetorically, sighing. While this all came on really fast, and I reminded myself I didn't really know who this handsome stranger was, in everything I did the rest of that evening, I prayed that it was. As my hand accidentally touched his when we both reached for the salt, I prayed for God to shield my heart from these feelings. When he laughed at my story about the cows escaping last year and coming back wearing Christmas garland they found in the barn, I prayed for His hand in this situation. As I looked around the table, no longer feeling like the third wheel to a couple, but imagining my ideal mate sitting next to me, I asked God to step in right away if this wasn't from Him. Because I was falling faster than Clint when I pushed him into the hay pile from the barn loft when we were kids, except this time it was my feelings that could get hurt, and I didn't see anything laid out for a soft landing.

*****

The next morning, I received a call from Trevor that he and Trish were back from the hospital, and I could come meet James whenever it was convenient. I didn't know all of the plans for the day, but it was the weekend, so generally our work these two days was pretty light. I told him I would be over right after I made a carafe of coffee, as usually weekends brought Clint and Jaylee by for a cup, not to mention my handsome visitor.

The morning brought my daily devotionals and time in the Bible. I searched the text for answers and prayed for my fast feelings towards, essentially, a stranger. I had never experienced feelings at first sight in all of my life, and this was something that I was struggling with, as well as wanting to run towards.

While I prayed for my situation, I thanked God for the opportunity to feel. "Lord, no matter what comes of this, thank You for reminding me that my heart can feel. It's been quite a stalemate around here the last, well, *decade* or so—ever since I'd been looking to date. The well has been dry," I laughed, knowing God has a great sense of humor. "I asked for a man and well, you had one crash land on my ranch. So, Lord, whether or not he's the one for me, which would be totally cool if he was, I just want to thank You for mixing things up. I spend way too much time with just Clint and Jaylee, so this has been a blast."

After my prayers, which went on to include Clint, Jaylee, and my parents in Florida, I had the nagging feeling that I needed to speak with them. They expected my call on the weekends. As I dialed the number for their condo, which sat steps away from the most beautiful beach ever, I considered not telling them what was going on, but at the same time, if they specifically asked me about it, I wouldn't omit information. I just didn't want to worry them and by the sounds of it, they might have freaked out.

"Yello—" my dad answered in his favorite way.

"Hi, Dad," I said joyfully. It was so good to hear his voice.

"Well, hello, Annie. Your mom and I were just talking about you. Our neighbor is about your age and, well, that's it. He reminds us of you." *Oh, really?* I thought. *Are my prospects getting larger by the second?* My dad continued. "His wife is twenty years older than him." Listening to my dad laugh, I thought he was about to set me up with his neighbor, and I shook my head in laughter. "So. What's my favorite child up to this morning?"

"I'm your *only* child. If you had more, I probably wouldn't be your favorite," I teased, stalling the conversation.

"Just between you and me, even if we had been blessed with more children, those blue eyes of yours would still be my favorite. You look so much like your grandmother that I couldn't love you any more, kiddo." My heart was full as my father professed his love for both me and his late mother.

"Thank you, Dad. I love you, too. And Mom," I said, smiling. "And as for your question, Trevor and Trish had their baby, so I'm about to go meet the little man. James Ridge." I twirled the phone cord around my finger as I spoke, leaning up against the wall.

"What great news! Did you hear that, hun? Trevor and Trish had their baby." I listened to their happy chatter.

"Hi, Annie. Send them our regards!" my mom's voice echoed in the background. "I'll get them a gift right now and send it your way," she said.

"That would be so great. I'm sure they would love that," I said. Pausing, I knew my dad could tell something was up, and it would be a miracle if he didn't say anything.

"So, what else is new, Annie?" Bam. He caught me.

"Oh, not much. Just the usual around here," I said, letting out my breath.

"Uh huh. . ." he trailed off, waiting. It was now or never.

"I met someone. . . Sort of, anyway. It's still very new and uh, I don't know yet if things will work out or not." Saying it out loud made me feel like I was jumping the gun. But the more I prayed about Jack, the more I felt like he really was the one.

"That's great, honey! Tell us about him. Where did you meet? The farm store?" I laughed, knowing that the chances of me meeting someone at the farm store were greater than anywhere else, considering that had been the only place I'd been going the last few months with our church pastor being sick.

"This is going to sound crazy, but we met here at the ranch. He um. . . he crashed his spacecraft kind of near that old well pump. In the flat part. Where the glacier used to be." I was never good at directions, and I was caught up in explaining exactly where so that he wouldn't book a flight, train, and taxi immediately out here, thinking that the farmhouse was hit by a meteor or something. But my father was silent.

"Annie," he said under his breath. "I know things have been quiet, and you're more than ready to meet a man, but I thought I took all of my sci-fi movies with me when we left." He started laughing.

"Dad, I'm serious. His name is Jack Carter, and he works for NebulaX. It was a failed test launch—we're pretty sure, at least. He's dealing with a bout of amnesia, but. . ."

"But what, Annie? I don't like the sound of this. He could be a criminal or, or, WORSE!"

"What's worse than a criminal? I mean, in your mind, where do you go from there?" He was already spouting off something before I could finish my sentence.

"Annie, is Clint there? I don't want you alone with this guy," he said, firmly.

"Clint is very much present at all times, just like normal life. Jaylee was here last night, too. And I'd imagine that Trevor and Trish will be roaming around with that little bundle of joy that I can't wait to meet…" I trailed off. My dad had always been protective and tended to overreact at first.

"Well, good," he said, exhaling. "You know I trust you, kid. That was just a little far-fetched to hear this early in the morning," he scoffed, while I looked at the clock.

"Isn't it like eleven in the morning there? I bet Mom is starting to make lunch," I said.

"I'm still on Wyoming time, but yes. I'm sorry for reacting a little heavy to that news. An astronaut—wow. You could do worse, kid." His voice was lightening up by the second.

"Thanks, Dad. Well, don't get your hopes up. On one hand, this feels like an experience to behold. I've met someone whom I probably wouldn't have ever crossed paths with. But on the other hand, it was only two days ago, and I feel silly for feeling this strongly already. Besides, he has amnesia, so…" I trailed off.

"He could be running one of those astronomy death cults, and you'd never know it," he interjected.

"Why are you and Clint so much alike?" I demanded, laughing. "But yes. . . I need to be careful. Keep my wits about me. I don't want to get tangled into something that's wrong for me."

"I know you'll do what's right, Annie. And you know I love you. Call me anytime, and kid?"

"Yeah?" I asked.

"Don't forget to pray about it," he said, softly.

"It's the only thing I don't forget these days, Dad. Don't worry," I said with a smile, and we hung up. What a roller coaster—though I willingly bought a ticket for that ride, I was also relieved it was over. The second I turned around, I saw Clint walking up to the porch with Jack. My heart felt like it played pinball down to my stomach.

"Good morning, Annie," Jack said with a beaming smile. He had a toothbrush in hand and motioned for the bathroom.

"Good morning. Yes, be my guest, please." I waved him off, savoring the interaction, while Clint went for the coffee maker with a smirk on his face.

"Good morning, Annie," Clint said in imitation.

"Don't you have a coffee maker of your own?" I demanded, tapping my feet.

"What, and miss *this?* That's no fun. Besides, I couldn't let your pops know that I wasn't here for all of these little gems of entertainment. He's trusting me to keep an eye on you." He walked to my fridge and looked for the cream.

I pressed the door closed. "What do you mean by that?" I asked, feeling a little betrayed that they had some sort of agreement that I wasn't aware of.

"Now, hold your horses, Annie. Nothing crazy, alright? I just promised him that nothing would happen to you. You're like a sister to me. An annoying, aggravating, short *little* sister, and here I am, keeping up my end of the promise. Besides, Jaylee is trying to mop the floors and if I step foot in that house while they aren't one hundred and seventy percent dry. . ." he trailed off.

"She's going to send you on a rocket into space with me?" Jack interjected. I smiled at the sound of his voice but felt weary he was talking about leaving. Immediately, I wished I could slap myself without looking insane. *Get a grip, Annie! What is your problem? He's not your prisoner. He can leave whenever he wants!*

"That's it, my man." Clint nodded and held up his coffee cup and took a sip.

"Mmm. Just missing that cream. If only we had some," he said, dramatically taking a gulp of the piping hot brew.

"I don't know about *we,* but I have some right here," I said in my best voice and polite smile, as I opened the fridge back up.

"Why thank you, Annie. You are so kind to share the cream that I milked straight from the cow with me." I rolled my eyes and laughed as he spoke. Jack, not missing a beat, smirked.

"If you'd like anything, Jack—please, help yourself," I said, locking eyes with him again, while praying at the same time. *Lord, lead me into righteousness, not away from You. If this man isn't for me, please change my heart.*

"Thank you, Annie," he said, staring back at me with his piercing green eyes. There was a gentleness to him that I felt without touching him. A strength that I saw without him showing it. A mind that—my thoughts were interrupted by Clint.

"Are we ready to go see this baby or what?" Clint downed the last of his coffee and stood up. I nodded, though his back was to me.

"Yes, you're right. They are probably waiting for us," I said with hesitation. "Would you like to go, Jack? They are just a short walk from here."

"I'd love to," he said, while Clint shrugged.

"The more, the merrier. Okay, c'mon, get," he said, pointing for the door.

"What crawled up your tail this morning?" I asked, setting my mug down.

"You know how much I love babies, Annie." Clint put his hand on his waist. "This little man is probably going to be my protege. At least until Jaylee and I have some of our own." He smirked. Suddenly I yearned deeply for a family of my own. A husband. A baby. I didn't look at Jack. I didn't want to associate these feelings with him just yet. The thought crossed my mind— did I feel intensely for Jack because I perceived him as available and a good prospect for marriage? I wasn't sure. Stealing one more glance his way, my heart dropped. I couldn't deny the attraction to him that I felt. Sigh.

Clint held the door open for us while we scooted out of the house. His excitement was contagious, and Jaylee also met us halfway there, with her arms holding a small quilt.

"I made this for him," she said, holding it out to me.

"I had no idea you were so talented, Jaylee. It's beautiful," I said, pondering the little intricacies of quilted stars, rockets, and planets.

"Thank you. It's quite fitting now that we have an astronaut here," she said with a smile and wink at me.

"I love it," Jack said, as she held it out to him.

"I can make a larger one for you, ya know," Jaylee laughed.

"He's already got enough space blankets, Jaylee," Clint interjected, clearly not wanting to entertain the idea of his wife making Jack a quilt.

"Space blankets. Good one," Jack said, as Clint reached over and gave him a high five.

CHAPTER 8: JACK

FAITH AT WARP SPEED

I knew the moment I saw baby James wrapped up in a blanket that I didn't have children of my own yet. This felt like an unfamiliar experience. While I longed for the knowledge of my identity, the only part of me that felt incomplete was not knowing where my brother was, but the Lord was giving me peace over the situation, and that pain and worry had started to settle.

Now, seeing Annie shed a tear over the beautiful child made my heart yearn for a family. . . with her. This woman was magnetic, and the amount of energy I put into staying a few feet away from her at all times to control my attraction was exhausting.

Clint and Annie bickered like siblings over who got to hold the baby the longest, while Trevor and Trish looked me up and down. Our introduction had been brief, as everyone had been more concerned about the newborn than a proper meeting that could perhaps make the Ridge family feel more secure about me being there. So, I did what any outsider would do in this situation; or at least, what I thought they might do. I cracked a joke to lower the tension and make them feel at ease.

"A priest, a reindeer, and a baby walk into a bar." The room went silent as all eyes fell on me. "And the bartender says, 'Great—another joke without a punchline.'" There were a few smirks from Trevor and Trish, while Clint busted up, acting like that was the best joke he ever heard. He finally relented and gave Annie back baby James to hold, to which she immediately started talking to him in a low voice, and Clint came and patted me on the back.

"This guy is a real riot," Clint said to Trevor and Trish. "When he crash landed over there, you know, kind of by where the salt lick glacier was? I told Annie, we gotta lay low. Let him figure things out before we make any sudden movements or phone calls. But now, I want him to stick around forever!" I could almost hear Annie roll her eyes.

"That is so not how it went, Clint. And thanks for saying that part out loud." She looked at me with reddened cheeks.

"I think maybe we should make a call. I mean, there are things I am starting to remember," I said, under my breath. Okay, maybe not a whole lot of things, but I know about Hank. I remember my parents. I remember the crash. These are valuable bits of information that have crept back into my mind; perhaps all it would take is someone telling me the rest and I can just pick up where I left off and one day will forget that I ever forgot." Trevor crossed his arms.

"I think I know what we need to do," he said, looking very suspicious of me, as he had from the moment I walked in.

"What's that?" I asked as kindly as possible, feeling as though I was at his mercy.

"We should go see Pastor John. He's out of the hospital and expecting to pick up services again in the morning." Trevor revealed a huge smile on his face as Annie stood up excitedly.

"Did you hear that, James?" Annie asked, whispering to him about the joy of going to fellowship with other believers.

"What great news," Clint said, nodding his head and taking Jaylee by the hand.

"He visited us in the hospital," Trish said, smiling. "He had to have a few surgeries, and one of them had some complications. But he's back to health now or at least to the point where he wants to be, to return to church. I couldn't be more excited," she said. The joy in the room was contagious.

"And, after service tomorrow, since the weather is supposed to be warming up, he's hosting a big barbeque, and the band is going to play some music. So, be sure to wear your dancin' shoes." Trevor winked at his wife who smiled and wrapped her arms around him.

"Oooo-eee! This cowboy loves to dance with his lady," Clint said, as he spun Jaylee around in a circle.

"I wouldn't call what you do as *dancin',*" Trevor said, as he pulled a few moves that looked more reminiscent of a medical emergency than swaying to the music.

"I've actually been told I'm a fabulous dancer. Isn't that right, Jaylee?" Clint looked at his wife with wide, puppy eyes, and she stammered and stalled.

"Oh, um, well yeah, babe. The nursing home residents really enjoyed it when you gave them ballroom dancing pointers on that night we volunteered when we stayed in Big Horn for a few days. I think I do recall someone saying that they give you an 'A for effort'," Jaylee shrugged. Trevor smirked and broke out into a laugh. It was hard not to; Clint was hilarious, and it appeared Trevor was too. I loved the camaraderie of this group, and it felt like. . . home.

"Just remember to keep twelve inches between you for the Holy Spirit. I don't care if y'all are married; this is still *church*," Annie quipped.

"Yeah, yeah. You're right about that. There are *children* around. Speaking of which, it's my turn to hold my protege again." Clint reached out and took the baby from Annie's arms, and she put on a frown. James let out a little cry.

"You've upset him, Clint. He doesn't want to be your protege," Annie glared. "He wants to take after me," she smiled and stood up, walking over to the baby in Clint's arms. "James, when you're old enough, I'll give you your first rope to practice ropin' cattle." Clint's eyes got wide.

"James—I'll give you a bb gun, and we can shoot cans off of Annie's porch." Clint looked at Annie.

"James, I'll give you a spare set of Clint's truck keys, so you can learn how to drive without worrying about dinging it up. That thing already looks like it's partially *totaled*," Annie said, crossing her arms. Trish stepped in and silently took the baby out of Clint's arms, whispering about it was time to feed him. Annie and Clint went on.

"James, when you're old enough, I'll give you a *pony*," Annie said, staring down Clint so hard that neither one of them noticed the baby was out of the room. "HA!" she said to which Clint stammered but couldn't top.

"I'll find something to give you that you like better, James!" Clint called out, suddenly realizing he was no longer holding the baby. "Maybe one of them RVs!" They stood in a standoff.

"Okay guys, thanks for coming by. It was great to meet you, Jack," Trevor said as he shooed us out the door. "And I hope you will be joining us tomorrow at church?" he asked.

"I wouldn't miss it for the world," I said, and I meant it.

*****

On the walk back, everyone excitedly chatted about the pastor returning to church tomorrow.

"You're going to love him. He's got a wild sense of humor, and I think you'll find his advice to be spot on with everything," Annie promised. "Trevor is right; we should tell him our situation and see what he says." *Our situation?* I wanted "our situation" to mean that she and I were together. As I contemplated what our lives could look like, I felt like I stepped into a black hole, as memories came rushing back to me.

Darkness all around. Smoke swirling. I'm covering my mouth as I run to the flames. "Hank! I'm here, Hank!" I tear through the barriers as I scan the crash for my brother's car. The car that we fixed up together over the years. The car that he was out on a test drive before his mission, as it was one thing on his bucket list that he wanted to check off before going to space.

The EMT's had him on a stretcher. "He's lost a lot of blood. We will do our best, you have our word," they told me. Seconds felt like hours.

"Was he alone in the car?" I demanded. Hank had a lot of friends; we were opposites in that respect. I was more of a loner. Because Hank was such a big part of my life, I never felt like I needed anyone else.

"Yes, sir, he was alone. He lost control of the car and hit that median. No other injuries reported." The EMT waved me into the back of the ambulance. As they performed some life saving measures on my brother Hank, all I could do was hold his hand and pray.

"My brother was in an accident," I announced when I came to. I had stopped mid-step, and I stood here now like a man who had just been turned to stone. Annie and Clint looked at me with no surprise.

"Jack, when you were sleeping that first day, you said something like that. . ." she trailed off. "I'm sorry for your loss," she said, taking a step closer to me and touching my hand. Her touch sent lightning through my veins.

"Is he gone, though? I don't feel like he is. I feel like he's still with me," I said, trying to keep my emotions together. I remembered the crash. I remembered the hospital. And now, I was waiting for the rest of the scene to unfold. Until then, I just wanted to hold out any hope that he might have still been alive.

"Want to go inside and talk about it?" Annie asked, pointing to her house, her hand still on mine. Truthfully, at this moment, there was nothing I wanted more than to go in her house with her. The temptation was great. But, I believed in a God that wanted me to overcome such temptations and keep mine and Annie's righteousness on the right path. I knew if there was a moment between us again, I would have a very hard time resisting her. *Lord, help me say no to this.* It's as if Clint could read my mind at this very moment, and the Holy Spirit answered my prayers.

"How about Jaylee and I bring a pitcher of sweet tea over, and we sit on that porch that Annie likes so much? Some good thinkin' happens there, at least that's what she always tells me. Plus, I can bring over my phone, and we can look this up on the internet." Clint smiled and spun around with Jaylee's hand in his, not accepting an answer either way. Annie let go of my hand.

"Well, this should be fun. I'm sorry—I am usually the perpetual third wheel and now we can't escape them," she said, with a slight tone of disappointment in her voice.

"I don't mind. I really enjoy their company. Almost as much as yours," I said, resisting all urges to wink at her. Staring at her face, I noticed the perfect fullness of her cheeks. The soft blush of rosiness that reminded me of the pink nebulas of the night sky. Her eyes were twinkling through her thick, dark eyelashes that stuck out against her blonde hair. She was as youthful as she was striking; I'd never seen a woman with her combination of features and for a moment, I studied her face like I was going to need to recreate it in clay. I lifted up my hand and touched her cheek with the back of it. Her body felt like it was trembling below my touch. The softness of her skin was like velvet. I dropped my hand, suddenly feeling indecent to have done so.

"I'm sorry, I—" I shook my head.

"Don't be sorry," she said in a quiet tone. "I feel it, too."

"What do you feel?" I asked. She pondered the question for a moment.

"It feels like I know you. Like I've always known you. Not who you are. . . Heck, you don't even know who you are. But it's a feeling where that part doesn't even matter. You are you, and you are mine." Her voice was shaking as she spoke. "I'm sorry; that sounds absolutely insane." She laughed it off, but her laughter felt closer to tears than joy.

"It doesn't sound insane, Annie. I—." My words were cut short when Clint let out a holler.

"Well, guess what?" he said, as we stood exactly where we had stopped outside of his place. "The wife is bringing over some of those biscuits she can just pop in the oven, along with her infamous gravy. We're about to pop off a little *brunch.*" Clint did a cringe jiggle with his arms; with the sweet tea pitcher he held in his left hand sloshing everywhere.

"Brunch sounds good," I said, nodding. Truthfully, I wasn't upset about the interruption. I felt like I was getting closer and closer to my identity, and Annie and I could pick up this conversation later, when I knew for certain what my heart was telling me now. What I felt like God was telling me now.

As we ate the wonderful biscuits and gravy that Jaylee prepared for us, I could tell that Annie was disappointed with the company. I wanted to comfort her and tell her that there was nothing more in God's creation that I wanted than to be alone with her, but I couldn't trust myself with this unbearable attraction that was racing through my veins.

After we ate, Clint, as promised, pulled out his phone. "Let's see what we got for Hank Carter, huh?" He looked at me while holding out the device for me to look at. I nodded, feeling hesitant. The lump formed in the back of my throat. I wanted to remember. I wanted to know. But I wasn't sure I wanted to see it on a screen. Despite the argument I was having with myself internally, I took the phone out of his hand and typed in the name of my brother into the search bar and hit "Enter."

"Hank Carter in a one-car crash on interstate I-80." I read the headline aloud.

"I-80? That's not far from here," Clint said, sitting up straight.

"It's not that far from most of the United States, babe." Jaylee patted Clint on the hand, and Clint nodded, sitting back normally in the rocking chair.

"Sorry, I just got excited there for a minute. Can you imagine, star slingin' friend, having an apartment close by? A whole life within reach?"

"That would really be something," I said to Clint, but thinking of Annie, who had been awfully quiet. Her silence was hurting my ears—the ears that longed to hear the voice of such an angel.

"What does the rest of the article say?" Clint asked, while my finger hesitated to open it.

"I haven't clicked on it yet," I said, a twinge of nausea passing over me. I wasn't sure I was ready to know.

"That's okay, Jack. You don't have to read it yet." Annie finally broke her silence, and it felt like no matter what was in the article, I was going to be okay if I had her.

"Thank you," I said, filled with relief of the pressure being gone. "I do want to read this, but for now, I think I should just wait. This feels like reading about a life that isn't mine. That sounds strange, but this entire situation is strange. But things are slowly coming back when I least expect it." Clint and Jaylee nodded, while Annie locked eyes with me. There was so much I wanted to say, but I felt I had no authority to do so. I was waiting on God's timing before I acted on something.

"Well, I better get some seconds. That gravy is just too delish, hun." Clint got up and went inside while Jaylee announced she wanted more sweet tea. It came honestly, and Annie's eyes lit up when we had another moment alone. But before either one of us could speak, a chinook wind gust came roaring past.

My borrowed hat blew off my head, getting tangled up in the porch railing. Annie's hair blew sideways. Clint and Jaylee's vacant wooden chairs were toppled over. But when it appeared that something was flying through the air and about to hit Annie directly, I jumped into action and stepped in front of it. The force of the object hitting me sideways, knocking the wind out of my lungs. Clint and Jaylee came running out when they heard me go down while Annie sat with a shocked look on her face.

"What in the Kansas, Louisiana, flying-house, Wizard of Oz gale force tornado wind was that!?" Clint reached down and extended his hand to help me up.

"He jumped right in front of the thing. Whatever it was!" Annie exclaimed, while Clint reached back down to pick it up.

"Why, it's a loose piece of metal. Where could this have come from?" Clint examined the reflective material while I groaned.

"Are you hurt, Jack? It looks like it hit you in the back," Annie was very concerned.

"No, I think I'm alright. It's not heavy, but it was just abrupt. I think I'm more in shock. What was that wind gust? It had to be over fifty." No one batted an eye.

"Probably more than that. I haven't seen flyin' objects since that time we clocked a gust of one hundred and seven," Jaylee added.

"One hundred and seven?" My jaw dropped.

"Yeah. That was a fun one," she shrugged.

"I think this is off your spaceship, Galaxy Guy." Clint held it up to me for a better look. "You must have had some loose parts somewhere."

"Jack, you okay? Maybe you should sit before you fall over." Annie stood from her chair.

"I don't fall," I mumbled, before I almost fell backwards, Clint catching me mid-air. My mind went in several different directions for a moment.

"Gravity hates you, boy," he mumbled under his breath. "C'mon, get in the chair before you take another tumble." I sat back in the rocking chair as told and felt my head spin for another minute before it eventually subsided.

"My apologies. I don't know what came over me," I said, closing my eyes but feeling the presence of all three of them surrounding me.

"I told you; he's concussed, Annie." Clint's voice rang through my ears like a bell.

"Maybe he is or maybe his equilibrium is just off. He's been through a lot," Annie said, holding her hand to my forehead. "He doesn't have a fever. Isn't that a sure-fire symptom?"

"I don't think so. When my brother fell off the boat dock down at Togwotee Reservoir when I told him I was going to go at an easy pace but took that thing full throttle," Clint paused for a laugh, squeezing the bridge of his nose, "he wasn't right after that. Heck, he still ain't right." Clint put his hand on my shoulder as if to say I was never going to be okay ever again.

"Isn't Jeff the smart one of the family?" Annie crossed her arms and gave him a knowing look. "Like, didn't he *just* get his PhD in biology?" She tapped her foot, waiting, but Clint just shrugged it off.

"I ain't sayin' he ain't smart." Clint shook his head. Annie laughed.

"Quit while you're ahead, babe," Jaylee said to her husband.

"I'm just saying that perhaps Star Walker here still needs a minute to recoup," Clint said, stiffening up and sounding more eloquent than usual.

"I agree with that, Annie." Jaylee spoke softly as she put the back of her hand to my forehead. I didn't mind her checking me, but it wasn't her touch that I craved.

"Roger that. We're taking it easy today. I don't have anything on the schedule, except a few of those fences still need mended." Annie looked at Clint. "You think we can afford to wait a few more days on those?"

"Nah, you're right on that. Trevor was hinting he wanted some fresh air, so he and I will tackle that. Shouldn't take us more than a few hours." Annie smiled.

"That's great. Thanks for doing that on a Saturday." The group started to disperse, and Annie disappeared inside with Jaylee as they gathered up dishes.

"Thank you for coming," Annie said, giving Jaylee a one-arm hug as she and Clint walked back to their cabin. Pausing,

Annie watched them until they were comfortably out of earshot and then looked at me but didn't say anything. The dizziness had passed me, and I was enjoying the cool breeze that brought scents of sagebrush and a sprinkling of dirt in the air along with it.

"I don't know how anyone stays clean out here," I said, trying to lighten the mood as I wiped my forehead that felt like it was coated in a light dusting.

"The summers bring a lot of rain. That helps keep the dust down." She sat back down in the chair next to me; we were just at arm's length apart from one another.

"A few minutes ago, when I toppled over?" I looked at her, and she looked down.

"Don't be embarrassed. You've been through more than any of us can even imagine." She shook her head and was wringing her hands. I reached out to her, taking one of her hands in mine.

"No, that's not it. But thank you," I said, smiling.

"Then what is it?" She looked over at me with her devastating blue eyes and dark lashes. There had never been a more beautiful woman than her.

"I had some things come back to me. Not big things, but about my mission."

"Like what?" She perked up, squeezing my hand gently.

"After this test launch. . . It's a one-way mission," I said, the silence between us deafening. She looked upset. "I was to orbit the space station first, once I broke out of the atmosphere. Then, I was going to travel as far as I could, with the amount of resources I had. There was no plan b. No exit strategy. Thinking about it now, I'm sickened that I agreed to it." I put my free hand up to my forehead and traced over the skin.

"Why did you agree to it?" she asked me point blank. And while I hadn't thought about that until she did, I knew the answer.

"Because it was my brother's dream, and he couldn't do the mission. They asked me to take his place." Annie nodded, but I wasn't sure either one of us understood the situation.

"I'm sorry about your brother," she whispered, holding my hand tighter. I looked into her eyes, full of sincerity. I wanted to put my arm around her. To tell her that she felt like home. That Clint already felt like family to me. But as I considered all of the things that crossed my mind, my brother's fate took hold of me.

"He was an idol to me. I see that now. I've never felt clearer or more in tune with God than I do right now," I said, turning my eyes away from Annie and looking at the clear skies. The sun was reaching its peak brightness for the day, and then the darkness would come once again. Another day, another night with only pieces of my identity. *Lord, whatever it takes for me to stay here. I'll leave the world behind if I get to be with Annie.* I was shocked by my own prayer, but after considering it again, it was the truth. From what I could remember, there was nothing that I felt an urgency to return to.

CHAPTER 9: ANNIE
HEARTS IN THE VOID

I poured my heart out to this man, and I didn't regret it. I was glad it was all out on the table. I just wished he had responded to it differently. Mostly, I wished he'd responded at all. But it eswasn't his fault that Clint and Jaylee came over when they did.

As Clint excitedly chatted like a child, showing off when company was over, I considered how I wished that Jack would have responded to me. Upon reflection, I realized that I was feeling a lot of temptations being around Jack, and it was not my intention to get him to stray from his path. I was not trying to be a temptress to him. I did not want to sin against God. So, I ate brunch in silence as I was praying as hard as I ever had in my life that I could have the strength to overcome these feelings. Like Jack said, he didn't even know if he was single. Did I really want to be that kind of a woman that led him into sin, if he wasn't? No. I wanted to be a godly woman who exuded the embodiment of Christ and His everlasting love. I wanted to turn away from sin and my earthly desires. Most importantly, I wanted to keep said desires in check for my future husband.

I prayed for my desires. I prayed for my heart. I prayed that Jack got his memory back, and we could live happily ever after. *Even if that was in outer space.*

Smiling at my prayers, we moved the party out to the porch where Clint started in about Jack looking his brother up online. I'd never been a huge internet sleuth.

Last summer, Jaylee tried to get me to set up an online dating profile. I didn't have any photos of me digitally, so we tried to take one, but all of them were awful. The hesitancy in me grew by the second and by the time we got a somewhat decent photograph, I backed out of the idea.

So, Jaylee convinced me to put in a temporary photo that didn't show my face or anything identifiable, but instead, a shot of me off in the distance on a horse. I agreed to it, under the condition that we wouldn't use my real name. But as soon as I joined the site, looking for available men in my rural area, my heart sank. There were all but three men in my generous 1ten-year age range and one hundred mile radius. Two of them I knew for a fact were distant relatives and the other? Trevor's little brother. As in, eighteen years old, still in his senior year of high school.

"I mean, it sure would be convenient," Jaylee snickered. "And you can't deny that boy isn't cute." I rolled my eyes.

"Right—he's a boy. A child. He might be legally old enough to vote, but I can't date a teenager, Jaylee. Forget it—unless a man falls out of the sky, I'm never meeting anyone." We both giggled at the thought. Funny how life works out.

As Jack took the phone out of Clint's hand, I sensed a hesitancy in him. Clint and Jaylee were egging him on, and he started reading something. As he announced the article, I held my breath and waited for the sadness to follow—the sadness I heard in his voice on that very first day on the couch as he called out to his brother. But something stopped him from opening the article. I felt immense relief and I didn't even understand why. *God, what are these feelings?*

When Clint and Jaylee went inside, another wave of relief hit me. I hoped to express to Jack that I respected his boundaries. I wanted to do this right, if it was even going to happen. And if it didn't happen, well that was a bridge that I would cross, relying on the strength of Jesus when I got there. But before I could express any of my thoughts or feelings, a rumbling of wind off in the distance made me brace for impact. Hats flew. Chairs fell. And Jack sprang into action before I even knew what was happening. When the flying piece of metal hit him, I felt honored by his heroic move to shield me from it. I felt safe. Protected. Admiration of his masculinity. And all of the attraction I'd been praying away was just continuing to bubble up inside of me.

Once everyone left and Jack took my hand in his, I let myself feel his hand mingled with mine. Just touching our fingers together was such an energetic spark that if we had been struck by lightning at that very moment, I wouldn't have noticed. I wouldn't have cared. *God, I feel like this is the man for me. I want this to be the man for me. Not just because he's here. Not just because he's drop-dead handsome. But because of this spark. This zeal I feel just glancing at him—this is what I've always wanted.*

Now, he told me he was remembering something. My heart skipped a beat. Remembering? Holding my hand? I yearned in anticipation for his words. But with them, he gave the details of the mission he signed up for, and it shattered me. I asked a question, because I couldn't wrap my mind around why anyone in their right mind would want to turn from life on earth.

. . Forever? But I quickly felt that was a harsh judgment of someone I didn't know very well, and I was reminded that this was a person who had been through things I would likely never experience myself.

As he shared that he was simply taking the place of his brother who was unable to complete the mission, I felt some relief. The love that they shared for each other was beyond admiration. Jack opened up, admitting that he saw his brother in the light of idolatry. I felt him grow distant from me in our conversation.

"Is that why you think you did it? Why you took his place in the mission?" I asked. He was silent for a few minutes, and I greatly wished that I could have read his mind.

"Yes. My idolizing of him led me straight into danger. I think God allowed me to crash and lose my memories just so I could have the clarity to see it." I swam around in that statement for a moment.

"You know that verse, Romans 8:28? 'In all things, God works for the good of those who love Him.' I think this is very much the case for you." His eyes brightened up even more as he turned to me. They looked *out-of-this-world* green; like the little stuffed green alien my dad used to have sitting on his desk at home, next to his sci-fi books. My mother had bought it for him at a thrift shop as a gag gift because he always thought there were things in the sky that nobody could explain. I thought for a moment how much my dad would like Jack, given his appreciation for all things sci-fi and outer space, and it brought joy to my heart. *God, don't let me get ahead of myself again!*

"You took the words out of my mouth, Annie. God did bring me here and stripped my mind so that I might see only what He wants me to see. And one of those things is you." He let go of my hand and stood, walking to the railing of the porch and looking out at the ranch. "I don't want to misspeak or commit any sins unintentionally, Annie. If Jesus says it is adultery to even look at a woman who is not your wife with *intentions,* then I need to protect us both from that." He turned to me, his sturdy, masculine physique feeling like it towered over me, and I liked it. "You must know that I feel the same way as you, but I'm fighting it until I know for sure it's not adultery." His words almost turned into stone as I heard them. I released my breath, nodding.

"I agree with you, Jack. It's just very hard to fight these feelings. We need to have clear boundaries. Could we just act as friends until we know more?" Jack smiled, but it didn't reach his eyes.

"Of course. Let's just be friends." He held out his hand to me to shake it, and I did, but once again, even the slightest touch of his skin felt like laser beams were shooting through my veins.

"How do you do that?" I asked.

"Do what?"

"Make me feel like. . . a woman. Feminine. Soft." My words got quieter as I went on.

"You are a woman, Annie." His cheeks turned the slightest shade of red.

"I know. I just mean. . . no *friend* of mine has ever made me feel like one before. Out here, I've just been workin', and hayin', and feedin' cows just like everyone else. But you bring something out of me that I've never felt before. And I just want to say, thank you. Even if this whole thing implodes. Even if it turns out you've got nine wives and forty-one children, like on one of those TLC shows. I'm just glad to have felt this feeling," I said. Not a moment later, Jack busted up laughing.

"Nine wives? I may not remember my relationship status, but I know for certain I'm not a polygamist, Annie." We smiled.

"You know what I mean." He nodded.

"I do. And thank you. You bring out something in me, too. Something I feel like I've long forgotten, since I've been too busy chasing other pursuits." He looked back off the railing of the porch, while the sun started moving slowly in the sky. It was in the afternoon now—that point in the middle of a Saturday in spring where you still have daylight ahead of you, but the day is not young. The time of day where you wonder where the rest of it went.

As Jack lingered, I knew this time was coming to a close. Whether he got his memory back or not, this wasn't going to last. Suddenly, I felt homesick. But as I looked around my home, the only place I'd ever lived, I knew it wasn't for here. It was for him. My home was with Jack. The thought scared me. I didn't want to be destroyed if this ended. *Lord, please step in and shield me from these feelings.* I just kept praying the same thing over and over; without ceasing. But the feelings persisted. What lesson was God trying to teach me here? I wondered.

Clint and Trevor eventually walked by as Jack and I were still reveling in silence. Clint was pushing a wheelbarrow with the fencing supplies, and Trevor had a branding iron. I stood up at the sight, hollering out to Trevor.

"On a Saturday?" I asked, in reference to the large amount of work that went into branding cattle.

"It needs to be done. Want to help?" I looked at Clint who was focused on his wheelbarrow. I looked at Jack, who didn't even know what we were talking about. I nodded to Trevor and waved him off.

"Ever been to a cattle branding before?" I asked Jack, who looked at me like I was speaking a foreign language.

*****

"Annie will be on horseback, and she's gonna be ropin' the calves. Trevor's got the hot iron brand, so that leaves you and me to hold onto the calf as it gets its brandin'. You get all that?" Clint gave a square look to Jack, who nodded in reply.

"We're going to tackle the calves, like in football?" Clint busted up with laughter.

"No, not exactly. We just kind of flop them sideways so they can get branded. It's like our proof of ownership of the cow." Jack nodded.

"Okay, I'm ready, coach. Put me in the game." Jack made Clint laugh again. I loved their banter. It felt very brotherly. Natural. *Lord, here I go again. I'm afraid he fits in too well, and I'm at the point of no return.*

As Trevor had all of the cows fenced off in a corral, I rode in on Whisper, my rope in hand. I waited for the signal, to which Clint just hollered, "Go!", and I started circling my rope in the air. When it was time to lasso the calf that was in my crosshairs, I got it with ease around its head.

Call me a softy, but I never yanked hard on the neck when I roped an animal. Just enough that it sensed it shouldn't try and run, but they almost always did anyway. Nevertheless, Clint and Jack jumped into action as Clint took the animal's head and neck in his chest, and Jack carefully flipped the calf on its side and held its hooves together. Trevor acted quickly; pressing the brand into the hip area of the calf and then Jack and Clint immediately released the animal. It was the easiest and most proficient branding we had ever had. And we repeated it twenty more times before the sun went down.

At the end of it, Jack was completely covered in mud and smelled like manure. I laughed under my breath, thinking that this was one way for God to help me lighten my attraction to this man, but he came about it so honestly, it didn't soften my feelings whatsoever.

"You didn't tell me this would happen," Jack said, as I got out of the saddle and led Whisper back to her corral.

"All in a day's work," I said with a giggle.

"But you are still sparkling clean." He pointed to me with his filthy hand.

"C'mon, bud. I've got a hose hooked up right over here, and we can take turns spraying each other down. If I even attempted to walk into my house like this right now. . ." Clint trailed off.

"Jaylee would string you up like a hunting trophy?" Jack quipped.

"Now you are gettin' it." Clint smiled, and Jack gave me a wink before he walked off with Clint. I stood at the corral, relishing in his display of affection, just hours after our conversation about just being friends. From where I stood, I could see the men hosing each other off. Jack took the hose in hand and cranked the handle on the well pump all the way up while Clint was more concerned with taking his phone out of his pocket. I watched with anticipation because I knew the pressure of that pump was going to be similar to a fire hose and as Jack waited for the water to come out, the hose pointed on Clint. It did not disappoint.

Clint fell backwards almost immediately from the force, letting out a girly scream in the process. Jack might have been an engineer, but he couldn't figure out how to get the pump to shut off, and the pressure of the water was too great for just one person. Trevor started to walk over to help, but through his laughter, he didn't make it there very fast. Meanwhile, Jack still had the hose pointed on Clint, who was now the cleanest he'd ever been in his life.

"Don't go drownin' him, Jack." Trevor managed to get the sentence out while the two men pushed down on the well pump lever together. "If you turn this on full blast, it sticks. Only do that if there's a fire or if Clint is on the receiving end of the water." Trevor and I had tears running down our cheeks with laughter, and my stomach muscles hurt. *I needed that laugh, Lord. Thank You.*

Knowing Clint, he could be traumatized in a five-alarm fire and be offering to go get a banana split forty-five seconds later. There were no grudges with him. And sure enough, after he coughed up all of the water he ingested and was able to stand again, he slowly got up to his feet and took the hose out of Jack's hand. He looked like a poodle after a shampoo at the dog groomer; *not right, but clean as heck.*

Once he was able to talk after the coughing up water subsided, he told Jack to stand still and watch how it was done. Trevor and I both looked at each other thinking, *Is he going to pull the same on Jack?*, but Clint slowly lifted the well pump lever only halfway. It was going to be a gentle stream of water in comparison, but still enough to pressure wash off the manure. Trevor walked off, not needing to watch as Jack got hosed down. I told myself I would look away as soon as I knew that Jack wasn't getting waterboarded. But as Clint sprayed down Jack, causing his shirt to stick to his very muscular body, I found myself unable to peel my eyes off of the man. His arms were more ripped than I remembered. He must have had an eight-pack of abs. Chunks of mud and manure were flying off of him, but I still wondered, *How did this astronaut stay in such beefcake shape?* His thick hair getting tossed around in the water made me wonder what kind of hair our children would have. That's when I realized it was time to hang it up and walk away. *Get a grip, Annie. You've just watched a man covered in cow poop get hosed down, and you are still finding him hot? You know it's going to take a lot more than regular water to get that scent off of him!*

As if on cue, Jack hollered out and asked if he could come shower. He was walking up behind me now, while Clint unhooked the hose with an unsteady gait. After that, Clint looked like he needed the rest of the weekend off. I smirked.

"Of course. Go on ahead. I'm going to feed the horses." Though there was a chance that Trevor had already fed them, I didn't want to be under the same roof as Jack while he was showering and I was feeling attraction, despite manure. It just wasn't the aesthetic I wanted to lean in on.

"Thank you," he said, and I turned away before he could wink or I could count his abs through his skintight shirt. "I'm just going to get some fresh clothes from my room, then I'll be in." And he walked off. Now, I had some serious time to kill, because I wanted to steer clear.

The sky was darkening fast. A chill came over me as the sun dipped below the horizon; there was still a warm glow over the ranch, but night was here whether I liked it or not. There were a few lights on around—just exterior lights at the Trevor and Clint houses and my farmhouse. The homes looked like they were glowing from within. As the sun's glow dissipated, the stars came out in full force. I went up to the loft in the barn and sat down at my telescope.

When I was a kid, my dad watched nothing but sci-fi movies, and our hobby together was looking at shooting stars or "signs" of aliens. We made such great memories that it led me for a few years into astronomy. I thought, maybe, I could be some sort of scientist who studies the stars for a career? When I told my dad—who had been priming me at birth that if I wanted to take over the ranch—what I was thinking, I expected him to be disappointed. He never liked ranching. He did it more because he had to make a living for his family rather than because he wanted to be there. We all knew it. The only passion in his life was looking up at the stars and admiring God's creation. But instead of him being upset, he was thrilled that I wanted to pursue something, even if that meant he would have to sell the ranch to someone else if I didn't take over.

Selling meant breaking the legacy. We all knew that if that happened, we could never get it back if we decided we felt particularly nostalgic for ranching. But my dad never let me know any of those things then. I only learned them when I was far beyond the idea of astronomy, back to my roots. Ranching was where my heart had always been. Astronomy was just something that I enjoyed with my father.

The day after I told him of my interest, he left early in the morning, only returning almost at nightfall with this telescope. He had driven four hours each way to get it from a mid-sized town, as someone was selling it. We immediately tested it out, trying it from all angles on the porch, in the field, and one night, my dad even propped it up on the roof. We loved that the best, because we felt closer to the heavens than anywhere else. So, my dad made a hatch in the roof of the barn and built the loft and together, we created the perfect place to admire the stars.

I watched for a long time, knowing that Jack was probably back at his place by now, but I was just enjoying myself here at my telescope. Then, the skies started to change and brought along with something else I hadn't seen since I was a kid.

In the night sky, I saw blue and green swirls dancing. Pulling my eye off the telescopic lens, I looked up, out the hatch. With the naked eye, I could see the vivid colors moving around.

Going down the ladder of the loft, I opened the barn doors and looked up at the most magnificent thing I'd ever seen: the northern lights. My mind went to thoughts of Jack, as I knew he would love this. I walked over to his one room cabin and rapped on the door, but no answer. Could he have still been in my house? Could he have slipped into an unconscious state again? I didn't know. I picked up the pace and walked around to my house and spotted Jack, sitting in the rocking chair on my porch, clean and dressed in fresh clothes. Relief hit me and also a yearning to sit next to him that I didn't want to ignore.

"Good evening," he said, in his deep voice that brought all of the femininity out of me.

"I see you've also noticed the phenomenon we are having tonight." I joined him on the porch, my legs trying their best not to sit directly beside him, but I failed as I leaned back into the chair on his opposite side.

"This is a G4 solar storm. We must have had a pretty sizable solar flare. The earth's geomagnetic atmosphere is thinning. I'm surprised we don't see these more often than we do. We certainly will in the future." Hearing him talk about science made me miss my dad. He would be eating this up right now.

"Have you ever seen them like this before?" It felt like a silly question because of his line of work. He'd *nearly left* planet earth. I was certain he'd seen it all.

"Never at this magnitude," he said, smiling and turning to me. "Do you mind if we turn off the outside lights to see better?"

"Oh, of course." He got up and opened the front door and reached in for the light switch. The second he flipped it off, the sky got even brighter. After he sat back down, we were in silence admiring the night sky.

"Look!" He excitedly pointed towards the west as a satellite flew over.

"Now, I really wish my dad was here," I laughed, explaining his love for all of these things.

"I think I'd like your dad," Jack said, nodding his head.

"Oh, it would be mutual. Trust me on that. He'd be treating you like an alien specimen that he wants to study for the rest of his life." I laughed at the thought.

As we chatted idly about my family, the sky grew brighter with flashes of green. As the stars sparkled, the beauty of everything was just too much to handle. Tears welled in my eyes, and I had the urge to pray. So, I did, aloud.

"Thank You God for the beauty of Your creation. If this is earth, I can't imagine what heaven is like." I wiped a tear from my cheek.

"Amen," Jack said, putting his hand on my shoulder for a moment. "This really is the most beautiful sight I've ever witnessed." I looked over my shoulder at him, as he looked back at me.

"This world is not our home," I said, softly. "We're just passing through on our way to heaven." Jack never broke his gaze as I used my strategy to keep the conversation on God as a reminder of the temptations I was trying to avoid.

"You're so right, Annie." The northern lights started to fade away as the darkness increased. After a few minutes, I wasn't able to make out all of the lines of his face as we sat out in the night.

"Are you hungry? I have a pizza in the freezer." My stomach growled as I spoke.

"Always," he smiled, the last of the light glittering off his perfect teeth. I stood, putting one foot in front of the other as I walked away from Jack, unsure if he would follow me inside. As I flipped on all of the lights, outside and in, he didn't follow. I let out a breath of relief. I didn't think I could trust myself if he did. I'd find a way for us to cozy up on the couch, which would lead to kissing. And we just couldn't cross that line.

After I turned on my propane oven and popped in the pizza, I set my timer for fifteen minutes, pulled out a large glass pitcher, and made some juice from frozen concentrate. Grabbing two glasses from the cupboard, I walked back to the porch with our beverage.

"I hope you like cran-apple," I said, but Jack had his head in his hands. "Jack?" He sat in silence as I hovered over him, setting down the juice pitcher and the glasses.

"I remembered my life. Some of it, anyway." He looked up from his hands with small tears welled in his eyes. "I have a dog," he laughed. It took all of the strength that I had not to ask, "What about a girlfriend?"

"Really? Where do you think he is right now?" My heart sank at the question. With his wife? With his fiancé? The options were endless.

"I think he's at some boarding facility. After this test launch, I am going to have to rehome him. I can't do that, Annie." The look on his face was dire.

"I'll take him," I said, before giving it any thought and in disbelief of myself. But, having any part of Jack here was better than none. My thoughts went wild as I considered it after committing; I didn't even know what breed it was. What if it was a wolf hybrid that would go after my sheep? Or, what if it was a chihuahua that would go after my ankles? I couldn't decide which one would be worse. Jack stood from the chair and paused. Then, taking one step towards me, he reached in for a hug. It was mild—only his arms were touching me and none of his body as he leaned in an angle to do so—but it still made me blush at his muscular embrace.

"Thank you, Annie. Bruno would love living here on the ranch." Jack's voice was steady as I considered asking more questions about this dog I'd just adopted and the circumstances of that. We released our hug and remained standing a few feet apart.

"So, um, does that mean you probably will be going back to space, then? On this mission with no return?" I looked straight forward at the buttons on his shirt. I couldn't look up at his devastatingly handsome face. Jack shrugged.

"I don't know if I have any other choice. I can't remember the terms of my contract, but I signed to it. But believe me, Annie, If there's a way out of it, I'll find it." His words echoed in my head and heart; I did believe him that he didn't want to go. Like he said, after being stripped away from his identity, he saw what a hard choice it really was to go and follow someone else's dream. But just the fact that he had a dog to begin with told me he wanted a chance at a normal life even before he agreed to this mission.

"Say, what kind of dog is Bruno, anyway? Not that it matters. I like all dogs. Even the snarling ones that foam at the mouth when they see me wearing capri jeans in the summer." Jack smiled.

"Bruno is a mix. I don't really know. I recall getting one of those doggy DNA tests on him before this, but I don't think the results come til around now." Great, a mix. Could he be a wolf-chihuahua mix? I shuddered at the thought.

"What size is he? Does he have wiry hair? And if you had to guess on the size of his incisor teeth, would you say they are like an inch long? *Or smaller?*" The thought of a little rabid chihuahua was starting to make me smile. It might be fun to have around after all. I could sic it on Clint whenever he came over. The thought of that alone brought me joy.

"He's about ten pounds," Jack said, making the shape of Bruno with his hands. He has hair like a poodle. And he's sweet. He always wants to snuggle." Hearing the longing in Jack's voice was contagious. This dog was a dream boat, and it made me want to jump in the car right now and drive to find him.

"Where do you live?" Jack closed his eyes at the question.

"I think. . . Bozeman," he exhaled.

"Bozeman!? That's only four hours from here!" The oven timer went off, and I jumped up, relishing in the revelation that his home was nearby.

"Really?" Jack asked, putting his hands behind his head. My stomach went sour at the thought of him leaving to go find his home, but I prayed for those feelings. After all, there was a dog involved now. Someone who needed him.

I tore inside, put on oven mitts, pulled the pizza out of the oven, and placed it on my chopping block. The cheese was bubbling like lava. I rolled my oversized pizza cutter through the crust, served two hearty portions on plates, and returned to the porch, opening the screen door with my foot.

"Should we start calling all the doggy boarding places in the morning? To let Bruno know you'll be coming to get him soon?" I asked, a little too worried about his dog. Jack graciously took the pizza and laughed.

"I think he's used to being there and if I remember correctly, I checked him in for two weeks. So, he's not overdue or anything." Jack took a bite of the pizza and looked like he burned his mouth, but kept chewing anyway, smiling. "It's one of those dog hotels. He has his own luxury suite, TV, and the staff are like personal butlers with lots of cuddle time." We both laughed at the thought.

"It sounds like he's in great hands," I said. Jack nodded.

"He is. Now, to just remember where my other family is. My brother, Hank. I know I can just look it up, but it's not the same as remembering." He chewed another bite. "You could tell me right now something true but if I haven't remembered it, it doesn't resonate at all."

"That makes a lot of sense. I admire you for not looking these things up, actually. That would take a lot of strength. All of this experience would." I looked back up at the sky, noticing another satellite flying by. "Do you think they are looking for you?"

"They? You mean, NebulaX?" I nodded at his question. "That whole thing is still kind of a blur but, short answer, yes." My vision of two men dressed in all black suits appearing at the house came roaring back. "But my beacon was completely destroyed in the crash. And I cut all of the wires to the radar system that day we went back. So, if they had been looking in that first twenty-four hours, they would have gotten a general vicinity, like somewhere in the Rocky Mountains. But after that, lights out. They would have to be flying drones over every corner of the area to locate a large metal object, like my craft. After that, they would probably assume I'm dead and start a coverup operation."

"What do you mean, a coverup?"

"NebulaX has a lot of investors. People who want to be able to take leisurely trips to space, like a vacation holiday. That's what NebulaX is exploring—space tourism. If those investors get wind that the very first test launch failed, and someone may have died—which, thank You Lord, I didn't— NebulaX is not going to fare very well in that outcome. Investors are skittish, and there is always the next space company to put their money into once they pull it from us. So, they'd probably spin the narrative that I got sucked into a black hole or something. That is much more desirable than a craft failing." My jaw dropped.

"A black hole? Space tourism? Have these folks been to Yellowstone? The mud pots look like something you'd see on Mars, and you get to view it from the comfort of gravity, and you get to live another day. . ." Jack smiled.

"I've always wanted to go to Yellowstone."

"I'd love to take you sometime. It's just a 90-minute drive from here. Heck, it was only a 45-minute drive from Bozeman." I looked at him with wonder.

"Don't think I get much time off," Jack laughed, but there was a tone to it that showed just how unhappy he was with his life.

"What if you just didn't go back? You can hide out here for as long as you want. Clint can go pick up Bruno on your behalf." My voice felt. . . desperate for a solution for Jack, who just smiled and looked off into the vast darkness.

"Wouldn't that be great?" His tone left nothing to the imagination. He was earnestly wishing that could happen, but we both knew it couldn't. "They will never stop looking for me. Not that they will do what's right when they do find me. But, it would be better to let them find me, so I don't have to hide. I'm going to pray that there's a way out of this, Annie." And as we sat in silence, looking up at the beauty of the creation, we silently pleaded with the One who made it all.

CHAPTER 10: JACK
GALACTIC GRACE

When my eyes opened in the morning, the sun was already up. "Thank You, Lord, for giving me another day," I said, as I leaned into my morning prayer. There had been so much good that had come out of this experience. Though it felt scary to not remember, I had felt the presence of God more than anything else. And that was a blessing I couldn't comprehend enough to be grateful for.

Today was Sunday, and I was to attend church service with the group. I was looking forward to meeting their congregation. I didn't think I had gotten to attend church much at home with my work schedule.

After the service, we were to attend some sort of social mixer with dancing. Recalling Clint's moves from the other day, I knew I was in for a treat. If this group was anything, it was entertaining. My thoughts went immediately to Annie. Would she and I dance?

Just then, a realization took hold of me. A memory so strong, I felt momentarily paralyzed. I couldn't even call it a realization, but more of my identity. "Thank You, Lord," I said, standing next to the window of my shack, feeling the sun on my skin. "You are so, so good to me."

I dressed in some of the clothes Annie lent me, taking extra time to ensure my shirt was tucked in neatly and that all of the buttons lined up. Stepping outside, I brushed my teeth, utilizing a water bottle in place of a faucet. I thought of Bruno, the memories of whom were filling my mind by the second, barely being able to contain my laughter at some of the recollections of his playfulness. Bruno loved toys more than food. He was interested in treats alright, but if you gave him the option of a bone or a fresh squeaker toy, he'd about rip your hand off taking the toy. Oh, how I yearned for that little dog, and I asked God to please make a way for me to stay on earth. I didn't want to leave. I didn't want to complete my brother's mission. I went back inside my cabin and put my toothbrush away.

Hank. The thought of him sparked some sort of idea, but I couldn't grasp it. Hank, where are you? I wondered. Up until now, I'd assumed he'd been gone, dancing at the feet of Jesus. But my brother was complicated. His earthly desires, err. . . his mortal desires did not really align with that of God. I wanted to believe he was saved. But, at the end of the day, I didn't know. Only God knew his heart. And from what I could remember, it was set on bringing glory to himself rather than our Creator. Something inside was nagging at my mind that Hank wasn't where I thought he was. And that made me feel ill.

A knock on my cabin door made my heart sink. I opened it up, expecting to see the beautiful Annie where I would share the news of my memories with. But it was Trevor.

"Good morning, Jack. We're about to sit down and have some food before church, and I just wanted to make sure you joined us." Trevor, holding his newborn son in his arms, had what I wanted. A wife. A family. A kindness to him that made sure no one was left out.

"Thanks, man. I'm ready, and I'd love to join." Grabbing the borrowed cowboy hat from the desk and my Bible from my bag, I closed the door behind me.

"Good morning, Jupiter Jack," Clint's voice rang through Annie's farmhouse. While everyone giggled at another nickname, my eyes searched for hers. She wasn't to be found.

"Annie will be out in a minute, boy. Come get some of this before baby James eats it all." Clint pointed at the platter of food in front of him. Steak and eggs. My stomach growled at the sight.

I did as I was told, taking a seat and serving myself a hearty portion of the breakfast. "Thank you," I said to Clint and Jaylee.

"Don't thank us yet. Annie made it." His teasing of her made me feel defensive. I thought the food was excellent. "I'm just playin'—don't worry. I know you like her," Clint whispered, smoothing things out. I nodded.

A door opened from the other side of the house, and the clicking of a woman's shoes could be heard echoing throughout. The room fell silent.

Annie emerged, and it was like seeing a mirage of a water fountain after crawling through a desert on my arms and feet. She was wearing a long-sleeved blue, paisley dress that came just below her knees and floral cowboy boots with a heel. Her eyes looked so bright, I thought they might be electrified. There was a glitter to her lips again and something light and shiny on her eyelids, making them look like moonbeams every time she blinked. As she took to her seat at the table, I felt as dumbfounded as I gawked. I'd never seen a more beautiful woman in my life, and now I knew that for a fact.

"Let us pray?" Trevor asked, and everyone nodded, including Annie, whose cheeks were reddening every time she glanced at me. I slammed my hands together and my eyes shut as Trevor led us in prayer, only realizing I was holding my breath when he said "Amen."

"Amen," Annie said aloud, as if I needed a reason to look in her direction.

"Amen," I let out in a barely audible whisper. "Thank you for having me." I wanted to lock eyes with her again, but for some reason, I couldn't catch her gaze like I had been able to the night before. Just twelve hours ago, we had been sharing a pizza on her porch while she told me all about her dad's quirkiness, and I shared about Bruno. At times, she had me laughing, and I couldn't recall a moment I'd ever felt so free. To be fair, I still couldn't remember much of the last few months of my life, but I knew it then, and I understood it now: There was a freeness to Annie that I gravitated towards. Her willingness to love, to feel, to experience the world around her from a godly lens was everything I'd ever wanted in a wife. Sitting around the table, being surrounded by a great group of ranchers who were laughing and breaking bread together, made me reevaluate my life.

Why was I chasing the dream of my brother? Yes, I'd been idolizing him. But it wasn't like he would cease being my brother if I didn't do the mission. *Lord, give me a way out of this if it is Your will. I have no desire to be lost in space for the rest of my days. I have no desire to even return to the spacecraft for another test flight.*

As we ate, and my mind spiraled further into the realization that NebulaX was going to hold me to this mission even though the first one failed, I kept thinking of Annie's offer. To let me stay here, to hide out. But that felt like the coward's choice. And I wasn't going to hide from them if they came knocking.

As breakfast wound down, the group started discussing the cars that we were going to take to church, and at least for now, I let the thoughts of work rest.

"Normally, we all just ride together. But with the baby seat and my extra passenger, we are going to have to take the ole' Billie Bobbie," Annie announced to me.

"Who or what, now? Are we sharing a horse to get there or something?" Clint busted up in laughter, slapping me on the back.

"Billie Bobbie? She's an old Bronco that hasn't run right since the day it mysteriously appeared here on the ranch in the early 90's. Come to think of it, it has a similar origin story to yours."

"A Bronco? What's wrong with it?" I asked Annie.

"Not sure. None of us are particularly handy with vehicles. Thankfully, there's someone that travels around fixing broken farm equipment, or we'd really be out of business."

"I could take a look at it, if you want. Later, I mean. I have a knack for that sort of thing," I smiled at her, ready to offer my services as she needed.

"Cool," she said, nonchalantly. "It will get us there; I hope. But I'd like that. Right now, it's my only method of independent transportation since my parents took their truck with them to Florida," she shrugged. "With everything else going on, and my mortgage on the farm, I haven't really had the means to dive into it. But these things are collectors' items, so I can't fathom selling it."

"I know what you mean. I have an old Bronco, too." I smiled, crossing my arms. Annie was delighted that we shared a love of the classic car.

"No way! I've always said there's nothing better than a classic car. The new ones are *so* overrated with their unnecessary bells and whistles. Heck, I don't need to know the time in China. I just want a vehicle with a body made of steel." I thought of the blue beast that my brother and I restored together with joy. Things were most definitely coming back to me.

"Mhmmm, anyhow—" Clint interjected, as Annie and I had a twinkling conversation about Ford Broncos. "We better get." Annie and I nodded, and everyone went for the door. She grabbed a jean jacket that was hanging on a coat rack next to the door. It had little rhinestones on the shoulders of it that made me think of an interstellar galaxy. She looked gorgeous.

I followed Annie down the pathway around the back of her farmhouse. As it was positioned with my shack, I couldn't see this part of the property until now. Sure enough, there was an old red Ford Bronco parked a short way from the house, covered in a giant red tarp.

"She gets parked here because the snow blows the other way. I don't want her rustin' out on me." I helped her pull off the tarp and set it off to the side. For good measure, I placed a large heavy rock on it, knowing what the winds were capable of out here. We climbed in, Annie in the driver's seat, and I was pleasantly surprised at the vehicle's condition.

"This is way nicer than you made it sound," I said, looking at the near-mint condition fixtures, knobs, and most impressively, leather seats that only had minor cracking and crazing.

"I attribute that to my dad," she said, smiling. "He kept it in the barn until we had to convert it into hay storage after the old barn finally collapsed two years ago. I hate to have it out in the elements, but until I get another barn built, or a garage, I don't have much of a choice." She put the key in the engine and turned it a few times before the engine came roaring to life. "And that's her problem. She can't start that well. But once we get her going, she's usually okay."

As I listened to the engine purr, I diagnosed the problem. "I think the starter needs to be replaced, and I'd bet on the battery hookups being loose. That's an easy fix."

"Really?" Annie asked, taking her eyes off of the ranch dirt road to look at me.

"Really."

"Thank you, Jack. I didn't realize you were so handy. You've really been a big help the last few days. Let me know if you want to give up your life as an astronaut to come and be an underpaid and overworked ranch hand." She giggled, and I stopped myself from telling her just how much I wanted to take her up on that offer.

"So, where is the church?" I asked, looking around at my surroundings. When we turned off the dirt road and hit pavement, a few other buildings came into view, but they were few and far between.

"It's in town. There is a whole little town about twenty-five minutes up the road. Just don't get your hopes up; there's a farm store that doubles as Clint's fashion outlet, a church, and grocery store. I only come in once every two weeks to get supplies, mainly overpriced produce or a frozen pizza."

"Where's the nearest larger town?"

"Well, there's Big Horn, Wyoming, about an hour from here, one way. That place actually has some things going on in comparison to our little unincorporated area; there's a few restaurants and a coffee shop. Big Horn actually went viral last year for a large storm that hit the area. The weather reports made national news," she said. That sounded all too familiar.

"I think I remember that. Was it the record rainfall that caused flooding?" Annie nodded, smiling at me with wonder.

"Yes! The dam gave out. People would have died if they hadn't had this young whipper snapper meteorologist on staff, Hailey. She moved to the area temporarily and was planning on leaving, but you know how that goes. Sometimes, anyway."

"What do you mean?" I asked.

"'In their hearts, humans plan their course, but the LORD establishes their steps,' Proverbs 16:9. Meaning, plans. We make 'em, and God decides." She grinned again. "The meteorologist, Hailey? Well, I guess she found a reason to stay because she ended up marrying the cowboy camera guy and now, they have a baby girl. We don't get cable out here on the ranch, but if the rabbit ears on the old TV are working just right, we can watch their weather segments. She had the baby in one of them once. It was probably the cutest thing I've ever seen."

"Do you want to have children?" I asked, holding my breath for her answer. I'd always wanted a family of my own, so I paused in prayer that she did, too. But either way, I knew this was the woman for me. Annie didn't say anything for a moment, and I thought maybe the answer was no.

"More than I want air to breathe," she whispered. My heart picked up the rhythm like a countdown to a rocket launch. "It's all I've ever wanted, for as long as I can remember. To be a mother," she paused. "And a wife." My heart leapt at her words. I, too, had always wanted a family of my own. I could feel it in my bones. I was overjoyed with the words that were on the tip of my tongue, as I opened my mouth to tell her what I had remembered, when she slammed the brakes as hard as she could, and we both jolted forward.

"Gotta love lap belts," I mumbled, barely having missed hitting my head on the dashboard.

"Sorry! That deer came out of nowhere. I hope we didn't, uh, further your concussion, if it's true you have one," she laughed under her breath.

"No, I'm fine. Are you alright?" I asked her, feeling a little queasy, but my head wasn't rattled.

"Yes. I'm used to that, unfortunately. But I'd rather risk whiplash than hurt one of the animals. It's a hazard to ride with me." She gave me a toothy grin and looked straight ahead, slowly picking up the speed of the road. I smirked.

"You know, I really don't think I have a concussion." She nodded.

"I don't think so, either. But you did say you liked me, so it's still a possibility." There was a sadness to her voice. "You know what, I'm sorry I brought that up. Boundaries. We're not going to discuss that until you know more."

"As a matter of fact," I started to say, but once again, my voice was cut off. Or, rather drowned out by the radio that was suddenly on full blast. Annie immediately reached to crank the volume down.

"Aha! It works!! It's been on the fritz for a year. Funny how it just now turned on. We either just picked up a good enough signal, or something else. I don't know," she trailed off. I was starting to think that this wasn't the right time to tell Annie the news. The fact that I remembered something very important, that trumped all other memories. Other than following Christ, this fact might have just been the most important part of my identity right now.

A song came on the radio, and Annie surprised me by belting out all of the lyrics. I didn't recognize it, but it had an old-timey quality that made me feel reminiscent. Of course, she had a beautiful voice.

The drive to the church was beautiful. When we finally pulled up to a large log building, I was admiring the mountainous country setting. It was sort of like my home in Bozeman, but about a million less buildings and people. I found peace in the landscape that felt new. The chatter of living in a bustling city, though not as large as some of the other places I'd been to—I considered how much that had gotten to me. But out here, it was God's country. There was no noise. You could hear yourself think. You were surrounded by the beauty of His creation. I loved it here.

"Here we are," Annie said, coming to a stop and putting the Bronco in park. The latest song on the radio was just about finished, and she waited until it was over to turn off the ignition. "Seems rude just to cut the song off like that," she giggled.

"Big Horn Christ Church." I read the beautiful, green sign that looked like it was painted by hand. There were doves on each side of the words and below, it said "All are welcome, c'mon in! Stay awhile, repent sin!"

"Pastor John's wife is an artist," Annie said, as she opened the door and slid out onto the dirt parking area. "But not a comedian."

Annie was holding a white, leather-bound Bible with her name embroidered on the front of it. I had the one I found in my backpack, and though it wasn't fancy, I remembered getting it as a gift from my parents when I was young. The worn pages made me remember more than just them; as I poked through them while we walked up to the church, I felt myself slipping back into who I was; who I had always been. I said a silent prayer as we walked up the steps and inside the church hall. *Lord, let me know the right time to tell Annie. And please help me find a way to get out of the mission. Or, if it is Your will that I do the mission, please give me peace. I don't want to hide from my mistakes, Lord. I committed to it, but now I wish to stay.*

The building was a few thousand square feet, more space than needed, because the amount of people who were here could fit in about two hundred square feet. Still, it was nice to spread out. I followed Annie, feeling the looks and smiles on us as we passed by large groups of people whom she knew. Everyone said hi to her, addressing her by name, but she didn't stop to chat.

We sat in a pew on the left of the pulpit, third row back. It was comfortable because from where we sat, we could see almost everyone else. As the pastor walked to the stage, everyone scattered to their seats, still making it in plenty of time, as he didn't go very fast. He seemed to be about late 50's in age, but physically weak. But once he made it to the pulpit, he looked up at us with eyes so bright that it was almost blinding. The Holy Spirit was in this man.

"God's not done with me yet," he said into the microphone, and everyone started clapping and praising God, including Annie. "The devil has been after me since I was a child. I've always been a bit sickly." His voice sounded laborious, but he didn't give up. "Many of you know I've had some more major health struggles over the last year. But all glory to our Lord, I pulled through and am finally healthy enough to be back here with all of my favorite people. Now, let's cue the music, shall we?" Everyone agreed; some were jumping for joy. Though at first this building seemed far too large for this amount of people—perhaps, forty people, max—it was clear to me then that the open space was filled with the Holy Spirit. The church was alive, and for the first time in my adult life, I felt like I found a home.

CHAPTER 11: ANNIE

RODEO OF STARS

Being back at Big Horn Christ Church felt like finding refuge during a storm. Pastor John had been here since I was a small child. He was like family to me. I couldn't wait to see him. Seeing the congregation was also great, but I wasn't ready to introduce Jack to everyone. I didn't want to overwhelm him, for starters. And then, the thought of him not attending next week and the questions I would get gave me a preliminary hurt to my heart. I was already feeling an ache in preparation for whenever NebulaX found him and took him away. He was physically in great shape, and he'd remembered a lot. I didn't know why they wouldn't take him on the mission that he had signed up for— that he willingly agreed to before we met. It seemed unfair in a way; he didn't know what or who was out there before he signed his life away. But I put those thoughts aside and leaned into Jesus. I was here at church. *Lord, fill me with the Holy Spirit.*

When Pastor John took the stage, my heart leapt. There was so much I wanted to tell him. And ask him. I wanted to hear his trials and burdens. But I yearned to tell him mine and see what he thought of this situation. Pastor John was very welcoming, and I had a feeling he was going to love Jack. . . I sure did.

As the music started, Pastor John's wife, Nicolette, took to the keyboard. We all sang with all of our hearts to the songs, including Jack. I peered over at him once, seeing that he, too, was worshipping with his hands in the air, and it pleased me, because I'd always prayed for a godly husband. Only after the music started to wind down did I consider that in a matter of seconds, I admitted to, one, loving Jack, and two, sizing him up to be my husband. *Lord, You're not done with me yet, either. Please don't let me get hurt.*

As the pastor started to make his way back to the pulpit, I was internally pleading with God. *I can't see myself getting over this if he is not for me, Lord! Please, Lord, let it be Your will that he is my husband I've been waiting for.*

"While I was laid up in the hospital the last few months," Pastor John started in, his voice sounding frail, "I had many conversations with God. But the most memorable of which was at the start of my stay. It was when I started to really consider the fact that I could die at any minute. I've made peace with that fact. It doesn't scare me, but what I mean is, we all could. Some of us will sooner than later.

"I used to think that leaving my family here on earth would be the biggest tragedy imaginable. And while yes, they would miss me—Nicolette would have to learn how to use the percolator for her morning coffee, and my kids would need to find someone to get that rusty Corvette out of the garage that I've been meaning to fix up for the last twenty years—but what about the hope we have in heaven? Should we, instead of mourning the loss of a brother or sister in Christ, be joyful that they are now in heaven, dancing at the feet of Jesus?

"Now, I'm not saying I feel ready to go. I don't and in fact, I just ordered a few parts for the Corvette last night. But that's me trying to take hold of my timeline. While I was laid up, tubes everywhere and needles—oh, the needles they have in the hospital rival a drinking straw—I really relented to the Lord's will. There was a tiny little bit of power I was trying to hold onto in all of my sick years, and I finally gave it up. I said, 'Lord, all of my days are numbered in Your book. You know what is going to take me and when. I am at peace with that. I give up the idea that I can control my outcome. You know what's best, and I want to live according to Your plan. Even if that means I go before I feel like I'm ready.' And you know what happened?" Pastor John paused. People started shrugging and shaking their heads. "I woke up again. And again. And every day, I felt a little bit better. When I thought I was on death's door, I finally thought I gave up control. But really, the Lord freed me from thinking it was ever up to me. I feel so light now. Completely at peace. None of this is in our control." He waved his hand around, looking stronger by the minute.

"So, my question is, what part of your life have you not fully given up control to God? And, knowing that any of us could go at any minute, are you truly living for God? Now, living for God doesn't mean everyone should go out and be a pastor. Don't put me out of a job just yet," he laughed, and the congregation chuckled in response. "But it says in 1 Peter 4:10, *'Each of you should use whatever gift you have received to serve others, as faithful stewards of God's grace in its various forms.'* That means you all have gifts, given to you by God, that will vary." Pastor John scanned the crowd. "Take Carmen, for instance. She might make the best cookies in the whole congregation. Once a month, she makes several dozen batches, and she ships them overseas to soldiers as care packages with a letter to each of them that she starts writing well in advance. I can't think of a better way for her to use that gift of baking. And I'm the jolliest recipient of her Christmas cookies every December."

As Pastor John continued with his sermon, I felt the yearning of my desire to be a wife and a mother. I felt that God was leading me towards raising children. I'd been a steward to the animals ever since I was old enough to help and while that had been very satisfying, I was ready to raise more than just livestock. My gift was going to be found in motherhood, in marriage. I knew that with all of my heart, and I was ready for the undertaking. Feeling at peace with God and His promises, I stood at the end of the sermon, and Jack and I shuffled over to the back of the building where there were no pews, and we started to mingle.

"You ready for this?" I asked him, and he looked at me with wide eyes.

"Oh no, what am I getting myself into?"

"Don't be scared of Pastor John. Be scared of all of the older ladies who are going to ask you when you're proposing to me." Just as I spoke, Donna walked over. *Donna was one of the women who tried to set me up with her grandson, Ken, a few* years ago. He never called but instead, sent me a few texts. I didn't have a smart phone and my flip phone, that I only looked at once in a while as I just kept it for when I left the ranch in case of car trouble, couldn't decipher the emojis. He had asked if I wanted to go to dinner over text, and when I heard my phone make a strange noise, I got up to see what it was. Everyone knew I didn't text, so this was the first to come through.

Instead of trying to punch three hundred buttons and text him back, I called him. Like, immediately. He answered on the fifth or sixth ring and at first sounded clearly put out. I told him that I didn't have a smart phone and didn't text. He groaned, but said he understood. I gave him my home phone number, which I swore I gave Donna before, but she was one of the people with my cell number too, so he must have asked her for that. The service was almost impossible, as I had all of one bar and was screaming into the phone. I told him to call me on my landline, and I could have sworn he said "okay."

Three hours passed before he called me on my landline. If it hadn't been a Sunday afternoon, and I was home relaxing, I would have missed it altogether. I answered it quickly, considering it could be anyone, including my parents. But it was Ken.

"Hi, Annie. It's me," the voice said on the other line. From having only spoken once before on a very poor connection, I was surprised at his confidence, as well as for the fact it had been several hours.

"Hey," I said, already feeling like he'd let me down by waiting so long to call. "I was expecting to hear from you earlier." I dropped that nugget in before considering how abrasive it would sound. Honestly, I didn't care.

"Oh, um, yeah. Sorry about that. I was distracted." It sounded like I could hear a video game going in the background, which I didn't mind per se, but I didn't love it either.

"Okay, then." I took a deep breath and reset my mind. God, please forgive me for being rude.

"So, would you uh, want to go out for dinner sometime?" I relented. With no other prospects, and no real reason to say no—heck, I didn't even know what he looked like; he might have been a real charmer in person—I agreed.

"Sure. Are you in Big Horn?" I asked.

"Yeah. I live right off the main drag. My favorite restaurant is within walking distance, so I can meet you there."

"Oh, okay. I'm an hour away from there, and I'd prefer not to drive home in the dark this time of year when the animals are so active on the road. So, would you mind doing lunch instead?" Silence on the other end of the line. "Hello? Did I lose you?"

"I'm here," blasts from the game were echoing on the line. Suddenly, the noises stopped. "I paused it," he said, clearly not even trying to hide his distraction.

"Well, thank you for your attention," I laughed. "Would lunch be okay? I have quite a drive and all."

"Yeah, sure. But I was wondering; could you send me a photo of you, first? I couldn't find you online." So, here I was, willing to drive two hours to meet a man who played video games during a gorgeous summer day, whom I could barely get a conversation out of, and before he could commit to me coming to him, he wanted to see my photo.

"Sure thing. I'll send it right away. I've got a really good one here on my flip phone. How about we hang up, and you'll have it soon. If you like what you see, text me back with the time and place, and I'll be there."

"Oh, that would be great. Thanks. My grandma said you're the prettiest girl she's ever seen, but you know, that's how grandmas talk. Thanks for understanding." I agreed, laughing it up about his grandma.

"Isn't she just the sweetest thing?" We had a few more cordial words and hung up. My flip phone didn't even have a camera. What a jerk.

I wrote that guy off pretty quickly, understandably. I wasn't opposed to a set up, but I at least wanted a man who could put in the effort of dialing my number. Now, as Donna quickly approached where I stood with my handsome, muscular astronaut to my left, she was moving so fast I couldn't even see her legs moving under her skirt. It was like she was a magnet in our orbit, flying through the air to get the goods on my dating life.

"Well, hello, Annie. Ken is still waiting to hear from you about dinner," she said, crossing her arms. *I bet he is.*

"Oh, is that so? Well, he required a photo before agreeing to have lunch with me, and I have no means to do that, you see." I put the ball right back in her court.

"I see. I have a camera on my phone if. . ." She looked at Jack, while motioning to the phone in her purse.

"No, thank you. I think I'm good." I smiled and let her wonder about this man that she was now enchanted with. I could tell by her eyes she, too, had never seen a man so good looking.

"Jack Carter. Pleasure to meet you." He held out his hand like the gentleman that he was. Ken could learn a thing or two from him.

"Donna Walker. Nice to meet you, Jack." She had the look of a deer in headlights as she remained shaking his hand a few moments after socially acceptable. Donna was a bit of a busybody, and I knew the rest of the congregation would be hearing this conversation word for word after the fact. She finally released his hand and looked a bit frazzled.

"Are you staying for the barbecue and barn dance?" she asked Jack.

"Are you asking me to dance?" He put his hands on his waist and chuckled, while Donna turned ten shades of red. I wasn't the only one susceptible to this man's good looks.

"Well, no, I mean, if *you really wanted to, I suppose—*" Donna's words were cut off mid-sentence when Pastor John came over and put his hand on my shoulder.

"I missed you," I said, giving him a quick hug and then turning. "This is Jack," I said nervously. "He, um. . ." I looked at Donna, who had her entire head turned to better hear my conversation with Pastor John. Thankfully, looking her way prompted her manners to kick in and she excused herself from the conversation. "Jack works for NebulaX, that space exploration company, and he had a failed test launch that crashed on the ranch last week. He's been suffering from some amnesia ever since." Pastor John looked at me with a cocked eyebrow.

"How very interesting! Welcome, Jack. I'd love to chat with you about your life and suffering with memory loss." Jack nodded.

"I'd like that, thank you."

"Say, I need some help getting a few things out of the barn to make room for the dance floor. Knowing Clint, we're going to need extra room because he thinks every flat spot is a place for whatever he calls those dance moves of his." I busted up laughing. Clint was a very animated dancer. If there was one word to describe it, I'd have called it *cringe.* "I'm afraid I can't lift anything for six more weeks. Care to help?" Jack and I both happily agreed. As we walked out to the barn with him, that was just outside the main church building and down a stone pathway, he started asking Jack questions. "What kind of memories are you grappling with, son?"

"As it turns out, things are starting to really come back to me today. They don't even feel like memories coming back now. It just feels like me returning." Pastor John laughed.

"That's great news! I imagine it was quite scary to not remember anything at first." The pastor looked to me and then to Jack with knowledge in his expression.

"It was. But thankfully, God has been there every step of the way. And Annie and her friends put me up, fed me, even let me borrow these clothes." Jack referenced the shirt on his back.

"I bet she did," the pastor smiled at me. "Okay, kids. Can we move these tables just a little ways? I don't want Clint breakin' a leg." We did as he asked and took the tables off of the parquet flooring that was laid out in a large square. "A few more people are attending tonight who couldn't make the service. Seems that the words 'barbecue' and 'barn dance' are more exciting than 'Sunday morning service'."

"Nah, I'm sure they are just coming to see you back in good health." The pastor shrugged.

"There might be a little of that, too. Any who, Trevor's working the grill. Nicolette is bringing in burgers and buns. Who wants to work at the relish table?" Jack and I both laughed as we knew we had no choice but to do it.

*****

The barbecue started shortly after the service. As Trevor flipped burgers, a few other men gravitated around the grill to help him. Jack and I sliced up tomatoes, onions, and lettuce, putting it all out on trays.

"Was this all pre-washed?" I asked him once everything was done. He laughed.

"Let us hope so."

As people started lining up to eat, we both grabbed a burger and went to one of the tables and ate. Lots of people shuffled around us, and a handful introduced themselves to Jack. He was very gracious with everyone, shaking hands and patting children on the head. While it felt good to be sitting next to someone at all, Jack made me feel like I was the luckiest girl in the world, and he wasn't even mine.

As the eating started to wind down, we got up from the table and took our paper plates to the industrial-sized garbage bin in the corner. As if on cue, a banjo struck a few chords and Clint let out a loud "Yeehaw!" while laughter escaped from Jack. Clint went straight for the dance floor, jumping and tapping with one foot, clapping above his head like that banjo was the best music he'd ever heard in his life. You couldn't help but giggle at this point, and I joined Jack in the laughter.

In moments, the dance floor was swarmed. It was standing room only, since it was barely big enough in the first place for five couples dancing. Now, with this upbeat banjo strumming and singing, it was a wild, two-step style. I held back.

"I think I'll wait 'til they tire out to dance," I said to Jack, not looking over at him.

"I was just thinking the same thing." Knowing that he, too, wanted to dance was enough to make me blush. Would our hands touch? Would we sway? It was as if I was back in the regency era, and seeing someone's wrist was enough to throw me over the edge. Jack brought that out in me, though, and I loved it.

Later on, the majority of people got tuckered out. Moms wrapped their kids in the quilts that everyone just happened to pull out of thin air in a church setting and laid them in the pews of the church or in the bucket seats of their farm trucks while they continued to mingle. And, when the next song that came on sounded like a crooner, Jack held his hand out to me.

"May I have this dance?" At that moment I saw my fate; there was no question this man could ask me with his hand out that I would refuse. *Want to jump off this cliff with parachutes made out of Walmart bags taped together with my childhood sticker collection?* I was in deep and felt a little emotional over it. While I did feel like God had been seasoning me for marriage, I did not feel adequately prepared for the hurt that this would bring if it couldn't be.

"Yes," I said, my voice shaking as I put my hand in his. I could feel all eyes on us. As if it wasn't enough that I brought a man to church, now we were seen dancing together. This was a rocket launch of a relationship status if I'd ever seen one, and there was a rough road ahead of questions if I had to walk away from this now. When we stepped onto the dance floor, others cleared out as if we were the bride and groom. A spotlight turned on above us, and I remembered seeing Clint standing by the light switches beforehand, so no mystery there. I put one of my hands on his shoulder, as he took the other in his hand, and we danced, with a good distance between us. It was a church, after all, but there could be a mountain between this man and me, and I would still feel the electricity of his presence.

My eyes rested on the buttons of his shirt, right below the collar. There were so many things I wanted to say, but I couldn't find the words. And the more I thought about it, it was nothing I hadn't already expressed. He knew exactly how I felt.

"So," he said, swaying expertly to the soft banjo music, my hand in his. "I remembered something else." My heart skipped a beat.

"Oh really? Do tell, space boy," I said coolly, looking up at his perfect, masculine jaw line and trying not to think of what it would be like to kiss him.

"As it turns out. . . I'm single," he said, my cheeks blushing wildly with the words. I stopped swaying to the music and pulled back, feeling like all the power of the wind had just been put in my lungs. The song ended, and I looked at him with an intensity reserved for humanity discovering electricity or trying their first bite of Nutella. Now, I was the deer in headlights.

"Jack?" A woman's voice I didn't recognize pulled us both away from the moment. "Jack! What are you doing here?" She was around my age, red hair, and wearing a pink dress. I had never seen her before in my life.

"Do I know you?" I asked.

"You took the words right out of my mouth," Jack said in reply.

"It's me, Catherine. Your cousin." Jack had a blank look on his face while I let out a breath of relief that this woman was related to him and not suddenly in line to date him now that he remembered he was single. *This one's mine, ladies.*

"I'm sorry. I'm drawing a bit of a blank. I've had some memory loss and—" he paused, letting go of my hand. The room was silent. The music man stopped, just as invested in this reunion as the rest of us. "Wait—Jill and Frank's daughter," Jack nodded in recollection.

"Yes! That's me! We haven't seen each other since we were kids, but—Jack, everyone is looking for you." Her words were both frightening and comforting at the same time. I would hate to have a family member missing. Now, they would at least know he'd been here all along, safe in Wyoming. But this part was going to hurt, I could just feel it.

"Wh-who has been looking?" Jack sounded uneasy.

"Your company, my parents, your brother, Hank!" Jack's eyes widened, and he doubled over, as if someone just sucker punched him in the gut.

"Hank is alive," he said to me, putting his arm around me and nearly choking up from the news. "He lived. He was in a coma, but he woke up," he said. "I just remembered." My eyes welled with tears at the news.

"Yes, he sure did. He's almost back to normal. It's been all over social media that you are missing and, well, I just can't believe that I am the one to find you. Here, of all places." She held up her hands and laughed. A sadness took hold of me. I wasn't ready for Jack to return to his normal life. But the joy of his brother being alive brought me peace.

"Will you tell them that I am here? My brother, too." He turned to me. "Annie, will you give Catherine your number so that Hank may call me at your home?" I nodded.

"Of course. Are you ready?" Catherine pulled out her phone in a second flat. I robotically gave her my number and turned back to Jack. "This is great news," I said, hugging him. So much knowledge had been dumped in such a short amount of time. Less than two minutes. I release Jack and looked off to the side, where Clint's jaw was nearly touching the floor.

A parade of emotions traveled the street of my mind. Jack was no longer all to myself and now, we were about to find out what was next for him. It all felt so much out of my control, and not a second went by that I waited to be reminded of Pastor John's message today about relenting power to God. *But it's so hard, Lord!* I pled in my mind. *Lord, give me the strength to lean on You through this and not my own understanding!*

After a few cordial words with Catherine, she dialed up her parents right in front of us. "Mom? Dad? You're never going to guess who I just found!" I found him first, I thought. Ugh, this jealousy of mine was very unbecoming, I scolded myself.

And just like that, the little cog was placed in the wheel, and the machine was in motion. This was fleeting. Jack was beside himself. It was as if our conversation we had just moments before never happened, and he wasn't just about to profess his love for me. And mine for him.

"What now, Jack?" I asked him, as he still stood at the edge of the beat-up, makeshift dance floor. He shrugged.

"I don't know, Annie. I guess we will wait for a call. Would it be okay if we left now? I don't want to miss it." I nodded.

"Yes, of course. Let's go."

We said our goodbyes and saw no need to fill anyone in on what had just transpired because everyone heard the entire exchange. The car ride home was silent. God gave me everything

I ever wanted in this hunk of a man, but it looked differently than I expected now that it was here.

"I'm sorry. My mind is going faster than the speed of light," he said, putting his hand on my right as I drove with my left. The touch sent more sparks through my veins and suddenly, the fears were washed away. Just having him touch my hand gave me hope that this wasn't going to be over now that he remembered things.

"So, is your memory pretty much back, then?" I asked, almost not wanting the answer. I was still feeling uneasy, and I didn't know why. He closed his eyes and put his face into the sun of the window.

"Yes it is. It really is," he grinned.

"In that case, do you really think that my steak and eggs were the best meal of your life?" I laughed in my attempt to lighten the mood.

"Oh yes. The best." He squeezed my hand, and I prayed that God would help this relationship endure if it was meant to.

CHAPTER 12: JACK

WHEN GALAXIES COLLIDE

The news hit me hard and fast, and as soon as it did, I remembered. Hank didn't perish in that crash, but he was in dire straits for the first few days. My memories of him in the hospital were from then. They put him in a medically induced coma so that his body could recover, and it was the most scared I've ever felt in my life. Until now.

Hank surviving meant two things: I still had my beloved brother who meant the world to me but thanks to God's convictions on my heart, I was no longer idolizing him to the highest standard. Hank was just a man and a flawed one, like all of us. Secondly, and perhaps most importantly, Hank being alive put extra pressure on me doing this mission. Due to his injuries, I was assuming he'd lost his medical for flight. He was likely never stepping foot into a spacecraft again and if he did, it would be the type that crashed here on Annie's ranch. And if left unchanged, it would crash again. Now, the idea of finding a loophole out of this disaster mission seemed very slim. NebulaX would rather me have died in a failed launch or died in space than admitted defeat on faulty mechanics and calculations.

I couldn't even look at Annie on the drive home. I felt that I had failed her. No, I *had* failed her. Before we even met, I signed my life away to space and now, as happy as I was that Hank was alive, I was done. Space was happening whether I wanted it or not.

It was clear to me now: The day I signed on to this mission, I had just come from the hospital where I was grieving the impending death of him.

All of the staff at Mercy General in Bozeman didn't expect him to make it through the night. In addition, his legs were broken. They said he had extensive internal bleeding. The injuries sustained didn't make sense for survival. I braced for impact.

NebulaX had heard of the crash and summoned me immediately. I left his side where I was praying and pleading to God for his life and went, no questions asked. That's probably when they knew they had me. I should've said no, I'm in a personal crisis. I wanted to stay by his side. But I went. And that was on me.

When I arrived at the futuristic high-rise, that the slanted roof always reminded me of a chicken coop, two men greeted me in the lobby and ushered me into the elevator. We went to the twenty-fifth floor, the highest floor in the building, where the CEO looked down on everyone all day. Where no good things ever seemed to happen.

"Good afternoon, Jack. I am sorry to hear about Hank," the CEO Mr. Yellowtail turned his chair, holding a manila envelope. He didn't stand, though we'd only met once before, so I didn't bother to go out of my way to shake his hand, either. "I've been reviewing your file. You have almost identical qualifications as Hank—same size clothes, same blood type. This poses an interesting opportunity for you to bring honor to your brother's life, if you want to do such a thing." I was in a weak spot. Now, considering what was offered, I should have just said no. Quit the company if I had to. Hindsight is 20/20. But Mr. Yellowtail was very persuasive. "You see, Hank signed up for an exploration—one that hasn't been seen since the 1400's when Columbus took the mast of a ship and discovered America."

"You mean a conquest mission," I said in an automatic response. "What are we conquering?" Mr. Yellowtail looked annoyed.

"However you want to look at it. In that lens, Hank was to conquer space." I was blown away that my brother hadn't shared these mission details with me. I knew he was going on a flight at some point, and it was his ambition to do so. These days, the rocket launches were happening weekly in preparation. All roads led to the company being ready for a breakaway craft that could be a secondary separation from the rocket. They said everything was a go. There was excited chatter. My job at that time had been in the simulator as the Mission Simulation Specialist. I designed the simulation system from scratch, and my team and I had run endless scenarios to pass onto the safety and risk analysis teams, and I passed on quite a load of data. They said all of my concerns would be addressed beforehand.

We routinely had all of the engineers run test flights, and that included my brother. He and I had the same degrees. We went to the same college. The only difference in our lives was that he had wanted to join the Space Force right out of high school, when I had my sights on the Marines. He graduated two years before me and when I saw him after his initial training, he was so excited for the work he was about to do. I wanted that. I wanted to be near him. So, I changed paths and followed him into the Space Force.

Hank never saw me as an equal. He treated me like I was just his little brother, even when I got the same grades and test scores as him. It was like he couldn't see past our two-year age gap, which was nothing. Twenty-three months in between our birthdays. But no matter how well I performed, he always thought of me as younger. Less experienced. Not a voice of reason or reliability.

When I voiced the concerns to him about the launches, Hank waived it off. He said that if I sent it to the safety team, things would be fixed. He assured me. So, I let it go and didn't think of it again until now. Less than a week after my mission failed and I crashed here, in Wyoming.

That day I stood in the back of Mr. Yellowtail's office, where I ultimately agreed to go on the mission, I didn't fully understand the terms. I was under duress when I agreed to it. There were many angles that I thought of over the last day that I could perhaps use for my own benefit to weasel my way out of this contract. But knowing my brother, Hank, he would never let *me do that to the company. He would say it was going to make him look bad. Cast shame on our family.*

I was at a crossroads. I was just a few hours' drive from Bozeman. My guess was that they would be here tomorrow to pick me up. My memory had been restored. I was physically unharmed except for the stitches on my abdomen that were going to need to be removed in a few days' time. There was no physical reason why I couldn't do the mission, but there was an intangible one: love.

Annie tried to lighten the mood as we traversed the roads back to the ranch. It was early afternoon now; the sky was already starting to dim. It looked like rain clouds were moving in from the west. We had some light joking about her cooking, which I thought was perfect, and I touched her hand. Anytime this woman and I made physical contact, I couldn't contain myself. I wanted to hold her hand tighter. To wrap my arms around her. To kiss her as deeply as I could.

Now that I knew we could do all of these things, I had a dark cloud of guilt hanging over me. Annie didn't deserve a husband who was gone all the time. I didn't know how I could be there for her. Especially with this mission, NebulaX called it "open-ended" because they put more value on distance we could go than having a way back. A way to get out of space. But they were so trigger-happy to get into space, they didn't care. I considered the fact that Hank still signed up for this mission knowing those things. My own brother was willing to give his entire life up for the company, and now it was on me to do so because of my own stupidity in agreeing.

"The biometrics are already synchronized. You being as similar as you are to Hank. . . Well, it would be an easy swap." Those were the words that put a pen in my hand and got me to sign on the dotted line. An easy swap. Part of me wasn't understanding the enormity of the situation. Most of me didn't care. I just wanted to get back to the hospital where I was anticipating the death of my brother. And in thirty-five minutes, I was back by his side.

His vitals were changing. The doctors and nurses had been rushing all around with IV drips and injections. He was intubated. There was nothing I could do for him here. So, I went home. Bruno greeted me with such excitement that I lay down in the entryway and let him run all around me, licking my face. It was therapeutic. I took a long, hot shower and made dinner for both of us, as Bruno loved eating pieces of steak. I prayed the rest of the night for my brother's healing.

The next day, the tone started to change. The doctor said he had a great amount of brain activity. His heart was beating on its own. His spinal cord was intact, and his legs were not completely broken but rather had a few fractures. He would walk again. They were talking in a future tense, as in, they expected a recovery. I praised God right then and there in the hospital room.

Another day passed, and I got a call that I needed to return to work. "Per my benefits package, I have seven days of family leave, and I'm using them now," I said to the woman on the phone.

"I understand that Jack, but Mr. Yellowtail told me that he would keep you apprised of Hank's condition while you come back and prepare for the test launch. It's on schedule for next week."

"Next week?" Sweat broke out on my brow line. I hadn't realized I would be in the air so soon.

"You didn't know?" Her voice lowered, and I heard her typing in the background. "Looks like you'll be gone for a week at best this first time. You're just breaking the atmosphere and parachuting back. Of course, for the next mission—" her voice trailed off.

"It's a one-way trip," I said, only now feeling the gravity of the situation.

"Yes." Her voice was sad. I thought of my life; I was single. There wasn't much to it other than work. But my heart broke for Bruno. I loved that dog, and he loved me. He was still young, around five, but the thought of him thinking I abandoned him was too much to bear.

A few days later, Hank was having record healing. They scheduled to wake him up the day I left for the test launch. I was sad to miss his re-entrance into life, but it was time for me to leave earth.

By the time Hank woke up, I was in the air. Thanks to my work in the simulator, there was nothing I didn't know how to do in the craft. My mind thought of Bruno, whom I knew I would have to rehome when I returned. I considered doing it before I left for this, but I just couldn't do it. The thought killed me. As the rocket got nearer to the atmosphere and I prepared to detach my craft, the rocket sounded like it ran out of gas. The window next to my seat where I was strapped in like a strait jacket revealed the flames were still present from the rocket. My heart sank. The safety precautions I had warned NebulaX about had not been addressed. With everything going on with

Hank, I had foolishly trusted that they would be. But at the end of the day, all that my company cared about was the investors. And they'd rather me have been dead in space, than have a rocket on the ground.

The system was in complete failure. I hit the detach button as the rocket was about to enter a complete free-fall, and my chances then would be slim to none. I called out to God for protection, and I only thought of Him as the impact of the separation made me feel like I was a shooting star.

If I didn't have a strong stomach, I would have lost it then and there. Pulling the lever for the engine, I couldn't get it to engage as I flew through the air. The rocket's engine wasn't the only thing that failed, clearly. Adrenaline was racing through my veins as I considered the fact that I might be meeting Jesus today. "God, I trust You!" I yelled out at the top of my lungs. The miracle of the situation was my craft was still upright. I could engage the parachute, and there was a chance that the force of that, though it would pull me upward initially, would keep me that way. The only thing left to do was to push the parachute button and with a prayer, that's what I did.

When Hank and I were little, our parents took us to one of those rollercoaster parks that were full of rides, rigged games of luck, and fried foods. Hank's favorite ride was one that felt like an elevator that was dropping below you. We rode it probably twenty times that day, but I never had the guts to tell him it scared me to death. This feeling was quite similar except in this case, it wasn't a carnival ride. It was reality and as I was falling, the sudden rocky air felt extreme. This was another warning I had expressed from the simulator. Though I wasn't an experienced pilot, the turbulence I was starting to hit felt unusual. And then I knew: The parachute was starting to fail. The fibers of the material were not strong enough for the conditions, and it was possible that because I had to engage it early, the heat from the flames of the rocket accelerated that fact.

The minutes went by like seconds as all of the bells and whistles inside the craft were alerting the alarm systems of the impending collapse of the craft. I could still feel the parachute was open, as I wasn't falling nearly as fast as I would have been without it, but it felt like I was being kicked around. Fear was replaced by peace as I prayed in those final moments, and the Holy Spirit was washed over me. I was going to meet Jesus soon. Bruno was going to be okay. My brother was alive; perhaps, he could adopt Bruno for me. There was so much left unsaid but at the same time, I was living for God's timing, not my own.

The craft steadied as I could start to see shapes and objects on the ground. I was filled with hope for a fleeting moment; the parachute steadied. My fast falling turned into a glide. But right before impact, the parachute felt like it finally gave in. I was close to earth. I didn't have far to fall. I closed my eyes and thought of Jesus.

As we pulled back into the ranch, I looked at the scenery with fresh eyes: The mountainous terrain was awe-inspiring. The animals looked like ornaments scattered around the fields. The grass around the houses and buildings had the slightest hint of green, a teaser for the season to come. I imagined summer here was idyllic. The storm that Annie and I rode in was the most romantically charged moment of my life. I longed to be here when the summer storms came. I longed to be Annie's husband, to have and to hold her for the rest of my life.

Annie put the Bronco in park and hesitated before getting out. "Things are going to change now, aren't they?" she asked in a low voice. It pained me to think about it. Every bone in my body hurt to consider that I was going to be leaving soon.

"Yes." I said, closing my eyes and putting my head in my hands. "When I agreed to this mission, I wasn't thinking clearly. I never knew I'd meet you," I said, but it fell on deaf ears.

She exited the vehicle, and there was a smell of moisture in the air. The sky was darkening fast, and I thought for a second that perhaps even God was sad in these circumstances.

As we went inside to wait, I slumped onto the couch and thought about this week. I could no longer feel any of my surface wounds that Annie had helped me right here. I felt like myself and in fact, I felt better than I had before, because God felt even nearer to me in the last few days without the distractions of everything else. Even with my memories back, I still felt Him. And I never wanted to give that up.

The phone rang two hours later, which in between arriving and the phone ringing, there wasn't much conversation. I knew Annie was hurt and honestly, so was I. "It's for you," Annie said after answering the phone, holding it out to me. The phone had a cord that was ten yards long, and it was curly and twisted. I could have left the room. I could have gotten some privacy. But I didn't.

"Hello?" I asked, not sure if it was NebulaX or my brother. The voice on the other end of the line made me feel things I couldn't pinpoint.

"Jack," Hank said. It sounded like he was as close to showing emotion as I'd ever heard him. "We found you." Except now I realized I didn't want to be found.

"The system failed," I said. "You told me that they would take my concerns seriously," I started in, not exactly how I'd planned this conversation going. I let out a breath; I was angry, and I didn't mean to be.

"And I gave them all of that," Hank said, in a low tone. "Look, they're right here with me. You've only been a few hours away this whole time. Can you believe it? We're going to come get you now. We hit the road as soon as we got word, and we will be there in about two hours."

"Okay, Hank. I'll see you soon." I gave him the address and hung up the phone, holding onto the receiver while I caught my breath. This was a whirlwind week—one where my life had changed dramatically. I was a changed man, and there was no going back. Turning to Annie, she had her back to me.

"So, are they coming to get you?" she asked, not looking at me. Her voice sounded high pitched and childlike.

"Yes. They left immediately after hearing and will be here in just a few hours." Thunder cracked outside, and Annie turned to the window instinctively.

"Oh, good," she said, with nothing in her voice to analyze.

We stood in silence for several minutes that felt like hours. Eventually, she sat down on the couch, and I went next to her, putting my arm around her. She just sat there for some time until she finally embraced me. The clock struck four, and I knew Hank would be here any time. Annie stood up, thinking the same.

"I'll be right back," I said, and I went out to the little shack they let me stay in and grabbed my things. When I returned to Annie's living room, my hemmed flight suit was laid over the back of a recliner. "Thank you for this," I said to Annie as I picked it up. Standing there with the suit in my arms, I was living between two worlds: One where she lived, and one where she didn't. The clouds finally broke, and the rain poured down, hard. We both walked to the windows, the gravitational pull of watching rain sucking us both in. Annie stepped outside onto the porch, and I followed. As we waited for NebulaX to arrive, I threw my pack over my left shoulder as Clint walked up to my right. Annie told him that NebulaX would be here any minute.

"You know, Rocket Man, you're really down to earth," Clint said as he put his arm around me. "I'm really gonna miss you around here." He wiped a tear from his eye and sniffled.

"You keep thinking we are having a moment. And you keep miscalculating that greatly," I said, turning to give Clint a real hug. I had come here by accident, but I had found a friend. The connection with Clint reminded me of the one I had with my brother, Hank, but on a much more even keel.

"I'll look for you in the skies," Clint said, pointing up and walking away. Jaylee, who had walked up during our chat, patted me on the shoulder and went with him. Annie went back inside, where she had her back to me as she watched the coffee pot fill.

"Annie," I said, taking a step back inside. "I'm sorry, but—" I stopped short when she turned around, her eyes filled with tears.

"Your call to duty is greater than this," she spoke softly, tears flowing down her cheeks.

"No. I mean, yes, in a way, but—" I couldn't find the words to say that I was held contractually to this, but I wanted a way out.

"No 'buts', Jack. It's okay. I get it. I'm thankful for the experience of meeting you and feeling this connection, because now I at least have something to look for when I wish upon the stars at night." My heart dropped. Was she ending things?

Before they even started? That wasn't my intention. But I'd always been bad at voicing my feelings.

"Annie, I still see a future with you. I really do. There are just things that I feel like are happening *to* me, instead of for me. I have some loose ends to tie up." I thought of how Hank would be in the van when NebulaX picked me up any moment. I hoped for a nice reunion. One where I could introduce him to Annie as a special someone in my life.

"Don't make promises you can't keep, Jack. You don't even know what plans they have for you. You might be never coming back." Her words stung, but I nodded in agreement. "I want a partner. A husband. A family. I want someone here, by my side; I yearn for love. As much as I want to believe that you see a future with me, and I see it too, I just don't know how that could ever happen for us." Her words stung, but I understood. The thought of being separated from her by time and space hurt me immeasurably. The truth was, I wished there wasn't this mission. I just wanted to return to my life as an engineer. With some creativity and better Wi-Fi, I could work from the hayloft right here at the ranch, designing better systems for NebulaX that wouldn't fail mid-flight. But I'd made some terrible decisions along the way that I was afraid I'd be held to.

"I'll look for you in everything, Annie. When all of the stars shine down on me, I'll think of the warmth of your home. When I'm closest to the heavens and far from the earth, I'll remember your smile, and all of the beauty will pale in comparison. And when I'm the most alone I'll ever be—far away, in space, in darkness—I'll remember your kiss." Annie had another tear fall down her cheek as I took a few steps towards her and took her face in my hands, kissing her perfect rosebud lips, electricity shooting through my body. Her kiss gave me life and at that moment, I felt God nudge my heart.

A screeching of tires, then the slamming of doors interrupted us. "Jack?" a familiar voice called out. I released my lips from Annie's, slowly letting go of her face and walking backwards. Tears welled in my eyes at the departure and arrival that was happening simultaneously. I was torn in two different directions: Hank, my brother. My only living relative. He was very much representative of my past. There had been much heartache. Loneliness. But also, miracles. It was a miracle he was alive.

Annie. . . Annie was my future. At least, if she still wanted to be. When I kissed her lips, I felt God reassure me that through this, Annie would be my wife. I'd been here a matter of days—not a season, not a long stretch of time—but I'd seen it for myself. The way she moved about her day, thinking of others first. How she cared for me. The way she loved all of those around her. The love I felt us share in that kiss. Above all, above even her beauty—which in itself, was the sun of my universe—was her love for Jesus. I'd always prayed that I would meet a godly wife and in Annie, I'd found that.

I stood on the threshold of the door while my brother came ambling up on crutches. "Hank," I said, nearly falling to my knees at the sight of my brother. He looked as though he'd aged a decade in the month I hadn't seen him, and perhaps he hadn't slept, either.

"You're alive," he said, leaning in for a one-armed hug, shifting all of his weight to one side to do so.

"I could say the same thing about you," I said. After a moment, he pulled back and got a good look at me.

"I've heard you've been through it these last few days," he said, looking around. "Where's the crash site?"

"It's way over there. Almost at the base of that mountain," I said, pointing yonder. "If it wasn't for this wonderful woman finding me, I wouldn't be standing here right now." I turned, ready to introduce my brother to Annie, but she was gone from the kitchen. Her bedroom door was closed and as much as I regretted not saying more a moment ago, I accepted the situation.

"We better go, Jack. These guys need to recover all of the parts and pieces to the craft. Then, you are going to go back up next week. Can you believe it?" Hank looked like that was the best news he had ever heard as he told me.

"Next week, huh?" I asked, feeling every bone in my body tell me not to go. Not to leave this ranch in the middle of nowhere. To stay with the people that I cared for in Big Horn, Wyoming.

"They wanted to wait, but I told them that knowing you, you'd want to get right back on the horse." He smiled and started to turn around on his hand crutches. As he slowly made it down the steps, I took one last look back. Annie was still in her room. Hank was halfway back to the NebulaX van, making a great pace on his crutches. There were two crew members in suits, no doubt waiting for me so I could come and do a "debrief" of what happened. Of what went wrong on the faulty craft.

"I love you, Annie. I promise you I'm going to find a way back to you." My voice didn't echo in the log farmhouse. As I stood there, waiting for a reply that I hoped so desperately would come, I felt a draft blow in from the back of the house.

"Let's go, Mr. Carter," one of the suited men said to me firmly. "We have a lot of people waiting for us back at base." I nodded, waiting for one more second on a reply that didn't come and left the home, closing the door behind me and stepping into the torrential downpour.

CHAPTER 13: ANNIE

FAITH IN ORBIT

I fought the urge to hug him, as if holding on to this man would make him mine. When he said he saw a future with me or he never considered me being in his life when he agreed to this, his words fell short. The fact was, he did agree to this mission and now, I couldn't see a way out of the black hole that was this situation. His duty. His contractual agreement to fulfill the dream that wasn't his to begin with.

I was filled with emotions, anger being the highest. I knew it wasn't right. I didn't want to hate him. I didn't hate him. Through reflection, my anger was directed at his brother, Hank. I knew it wasn't right and for a moment, I didn't care. Then, I relinquished it to God and asked for forgiveness for my feelings. I asked for a change of heart. I reflected on all the ways that God had shown me He heard my prayers—just having Jack crash land here like an alien was the biggest demonstration of that. I felt my heart start to soften into sadness.

I couldn't stay there and listen to his reunion with his brother or his mission details. My heart couldn't take the words he'd say. Would it be about how happy he was to be back with NebulaX? About how much he looked forward to his one-way trip to space? Or, how ready he was to leave all of this behind? So, I snuck off to my room while he was preoccupied with his brother, jumped out the back window, and walked to the barn, getting monumentally drenched in the process. The rain gave me crazy thoughts: Should I run back to him and give him another kiss goodbye? Plead with him to stay? To choose me over duty? "Where you go I will go, and where you stay I will stay," Ruth 1:16. I practiced my words with all of my heart, but my feet kept moving forward in the wrong direction.

Up the loft ladder, into the corner where the trap door on the roof was, I was creaking the crank open as far as it would go. And I waited for the sun to go down, for the stars to reveal themselves in all of their sparkling glory. And I cried. For myself, for Jack. When I heard the van leave shortly after getting up here, the tears turned into a river. I searched for God in the gently darkening sky of spring; the days were getting longer, and this sunset hesitated on letting go. I waited, the feeling of his kiss still lingering on my lips. And when the sun finally did set and the darkness came, I thanked God for the experience, just like I told Jack.

Meeting Jack was worth the pain of losing him. The far too brief love story we had was something I had yearned for. Though it was not the ending I had been praying for, I trusted that God was going to work this out for His glory, just as He'd always done. Because the same God who heard my prayers of loneliness, my despair of not meeting anyone, dropped a handsome astronaut into my life via crash landing. God had shown me again and again that He loves me, cares for me, and I didn't think He was going to stop now that I'd had a brush with love.

Sitting in my chair, I closed one eye, leaning the other into the eyepiece of the telescope. Through my teary-eyed vision, I saw a bounty of stars and was reminded of the first verse in the Bible. "In the beginning God created the heavens and the earth," Genesis 1:1. God created all of this for us to look at. I moved my telescope towards the moon, studying the craters and the shadows, and I got lost in my small-scale exploration of the universe. Just then, a shooting star went by in the glorious night sky. Here I was, under the same moon and stars as the man whom I loved and yet, we might as well have been worlds apart. Still, through my pain, as I looked up at the night sky, I wondered if Jack was looking at it, too.

*****

For the next several nights, I was up in my loft, sitting in the solitude and finding the peace of the Lord. On the second night, I saw another shooting star. On the third night, the moon looked irregular, as it was now in the waning cycle. I looked for things that I didn't understand and waited for God to give the answers.

"Lord, I have never once in my life looked for a husband in the stars, but I am wondering if after this experience, mine could be up there?" I actually laughed at the thought, which felt good. Laughter is healing. So, I laughed some more, knowing that God had a sense of humor in all of this was comforting, too.

After nearly a week, when I was walking back into my farmhouse where I would continue my ritual of crying myself to sleep, I felt the Lord nudge me. Truthfully, I was feeling stronger. Now, I'd been without Jack longer than I'd been with him. I was starting to wonder if all of it had been a dream. It sure felt like a dream—a drop-dead, handsome astronaut with perfect abs and a natural cowboy swagger? Who was also a super smart engineer who loved to dance and loved Jesus with all of his heart? That was greater than a dream. Greater than any fiction I'd ever heard of. The combination of us—him, and me being a Wyoming born and raised cowgirl—was just too good. I didn't know what step in life I could have ever taken to meet him in another way. Or, how our lives would ever mesh together realistically. My life was here, in Wyoming. He was out there, in the stars.

That night, instead of letting myself be overtaken with fresh tears, I went in the house and put a movie on. I reached for my dad's collection and decided on one about aliens invading earth. At first, I thought I must have been a glutton for punishment, but as I started to unwind into the movie, I was having a ball. I got up halfway through the opening scene and made popcorn on the stove and grabbed a root beer from the fridge. As I was watching the movie while lying on the couch, I saw an alien bobble head that someone sat on the railing of my porch, and it made me smile. I'd been so distant this week from the people whom I considered family. They understood and had been doing their part to shield me from more pain by not bringing Jack up, but I had decided that I was ready to continue living my life. Jack was probably up in space again by now. I still had people here on earth whom I loved.

Pausing the movie, I was feeling moved by the Holy Spirit to reach out to said loved ones. The first number I dialed was Clint.

"Yellow!"

"Not you, too?" I giggled at him copying how my dad answered the phone. "Except you need to drop the 'w.' It's more of a *yell-o.*" Correcting him brought some life back into my veins, as sorry as that sounded. Without the banter, I didn't think Clint would be happy. He thrived on it.

"Yeah, yeah, yeah. What's happenin', Annie?" I heard Jaylee scramble to the phone.

"Hi, Annie," she said.

"Hi guys. I just wanted to say thank you for being so easy on me the last few days. That's all."

"Mhmmm. But of course." Clint rolled it off.

"And nice touch on your little alien buddy on my porch."

"What alien? Is there another alien?" Clint's voice dropped low.

"Yeah—the bobble head you put on the railing. It's going to drown in all of this rain that we're getting this week. This might be the wettest spring I've ever been through."

"Oh, *that* alien. I just knew you liked those kinds of men that fly around space, so when I saw it at the farm store, I knew you had to have it." It sounded like Jaylee smacked him upside the head with the phone as he yelled out, "Owwww!"

"Sorry, Annie. Clint is, well, Clint." Her voice sounded very apologetic. Truthfully, bringing Jack up didn't hurt. I actually found it funny, and I started to laugh. Uncontrollably.

"Is she laughing or crying?" Clint asked Jaylee.

"The emotions are all too close these days," I squeaked out. "I've lost the plot. Truly. Anyway, I'm excited to go to church tomorrow. I'm going to take my car in so I can do some errands afterwards."

"That sounds great, Annie. We'll see you there." I hung up and next called my parents in Florida.

"I hope it's not too late to call," I said sheepishly the moment they answered. It was close to nine at night there.

"Never too late for our girl," my dad said in his smooth, leathery voice. Oh, how I missed them. "What do I owe the pleasure of your call?" he asked.

"I'm watching one of your sci-fi flicks, eating popcorn, and drinking root beer. Your three favorite things. And I just had to call to tell you that I love you." The words came straight from my heart. My mom picked up the second phone and jumped on the line.

"Annie?" she asked.

"Yeah, Mom. I'm good here, just calling because I miss you both."

"Well, isn't that sweet! We miss you, too. In fact, I was just booking a couple flights out there to spend some time. Would that work for you if we came out, say, next month for two weeks? We don't want to cramp your style, but it sure looks like the weather is getting nice. We don't have to exist in anything below fifty degrees anymore." Hearing my mom say that they were coming out was music to my ears.

"I would love nothing more than having you both here! Yes. Please come out!" I was cheering through my words.

"We look forward to it, dear. Now, the last we spoke, it sounded like you were living in a sci-fi movie." I could hear my dad sink into a cozy recliner as he spoke.

"Well, that didn't really work out, I'm afraid. He's on his way back to space. He's going to be on a one-way mission eventually. I did agree to take his dog. A poodle mix." Saying it out loud made me both excited and nervous, as I wondered who would be bringing the dog to me. I told him the rest of the details as he pressed to know the facts, and it wasn't until I was done that I realized my mother had still been on the phone all the while.

"You've been through a lot, dear," she said.

"Say, there's a new observatory here, just a few miles from our place. How about when the cows move to their summer pasture, you come out here for a few weeks? Get your mind off of things. We can look at the stars through this super telescope. I hear you get so up close, you can see stubble on the chin of the man on the moon," my dad offered.

"Maybe. That would be fun. But summer is the best time to be out here. You know that," I teased. They did know that. The weather was perfect. Not too hot and zero humidity. I suspected greatly that was why they were coming.

"True. Well, maybe for the holidays one year. I sure would enjoy having you out here, kiddo."

"Thanks, Dad. We will plan it. I promise. For now, why don't you bring your latest and greatest alien movies, and it will be just like old times?" He couldn't pass that offer up. The phone receiver felt warm against my ear, and we said our goodbyes and hung up. My parents were coming, and that gave me something to look forward to. I didn't realize just how much I needed that.

I turned back on the movie and grabbed a handful of popcorn.

*****

The next morning at church, I got there a few minutes early in hopes of catching Pastor John. I was excited when I saw him sweeping up the pulpit area.

"Pastor John," I said, feeling like fresh tears were coming behind my eyes. "I was hoping I could chat with you." He looked at me, looked around me, and then back to me. I knew he was looking for Jack.

"Well hello, Annie. Sure. I could use a sweeping buddy. There's an extra broom right over there." He pointed to a red broom pushed up against the corner. The small stage area was covered in hay. "Some of the 4-H kids used this area last night for their awards ceremony. They said no animals would be here, but they must have rolled around in the barns beforehand." I started sweeping, and he stopped, leaned on his broom and looked at me expectantly. Standing in a pile of hay, I poured my heart out and told him everything that had happened in the last week. When I was done, I was expecting him to look like the wind had blown his hair back but instead, he just smiled.

"Well? What do you think?" I asked him, and he looked back at the broom in my hand. I nodded and started sweeping again.

"What do I think? Annie, what do *you* think?" His question put me on my toes.

"Well. . . I think that I am just happy to have met him and experienced the love, even if it was short lived. . ." I trailed off, realizing I had no idea what I thought of it. God had softened the blow of my heart, and it didn't hurt as much today as it did yesterday. And that was about the only thing I was certain of. I shared with him as much. The pastor was silent for some time as we swept the floor in tandem.

"There are few things I understand in life, Annie. God created the heavens and the earth." The pastor held up numbers on his fingers as he spoke. "He sent His one and only son, Jesus Christ, to said earth, and Jesus died for our sins. And lastly, something I just saw last week, is that man is head over heels in love with you. Give him some time, Annie. Trust God in the waiting." And with that, the pastor smiled, gave me a squeeze on the arm, and pushed his broom off the stage, a big heaping pile of hay along with it.

I was left stunned. I didn't know what I was expecting—maybe some biblical advice on astronauts? But instead, my pastor told me to wait. Waiting wasn't anything I wanted to do, though. Who wants to wait? *A season of waiting.* I remember a woman at church saying that once as she expressed her struggle with infertility.

In the scheme of things, I was extremely blessed to have this as my biggest current struggle, and I felt that. I finished sweeping my area and went to have a seat in the pews while I waited for the service to begin.

After church, I left before anyone could ask me questions. I hopped in my Bronco, which thankfully started right up. It was running amazingly today, and I laughed that maybe all it needed was for someone to diagnose its problems.

After a quick run into the small grocery store for a few essentials, including a gallon of mint chocolate chip ice cream to drown the rest of my sorrows in, I went home.

That afternoon, Clint and Jaylee stopped by with a big, fresh bowl of fruit and a large plate of sizzling bacon.

"We thought it would be fun to do a little brunch," Clint said, his arms full as Jaylee juggled a pitcher of fresh squeezed orange juice. The bacon smelled intoxicating, and I was jonesing for some fresh fruit.

"Brunch? It's one in the afternoon. You just like to say *brunch,*" I teased, motioning for them to come in.

"You got me there. Makes me feel *boujee.*" Since they had kept some distance from me in the last few days, now, seeing Clint made me realize my body had been in withdrawals from having no one to banter with.

"You better have washed your hands before chopping the fruit. I've seen you out there shoving manure without gloves on." And just like that, I was back.

As we sat down, Trevor and Trish brought James by, Trevor carrying a big plate of eggs and potatoes. Trish was wearing James in one of those front carriers. There was nothing more than this, I thought. I was surrounded by people who loved me enough to organize this brunch for me and the God who loved me enough to provide all of this food and friendship. Even with the seat next to me still empty after all these years, I was so beyond blessed and grateful.

As we ate, Trish was telling us all the cute things that James had been doing, showing me pictures on her phone. They were mostly of him sleeping and occasionally opening his eyes for a little smile, but she was right—everything was adorable. As she was swiping through the pictures, her phone dinged. Then, Clint's phone dinged. Then, Jaylee's. I was the only one in the room without a smart phone. Call me old fashioned, but it wouldn't have worked unless I was at home anyway, and I had a landline. I turned to it, expecting it to ring with all of this phone activity happening. It didn't and when I turned back, everyone was deeply immersed into their phones.

"Okay, guys. What does the weather alert say? Hurricane winds? Torrential downpour? Oh, I know. We're getting twelve inches of snow tonight!" Clint looked up and shook his head.

"Nah, Annie. It ain't that." He looked back at his screen, scrolling a little more.

"Then what is it? Come on, guys. Fill me in here." I looked at Trevor, who must have left his phone at home because he was eating a piece of thick-cut bacon and shrugged.

"Yeah, what is it?"

"It's a news alert from NebulaX," Jaylee announced. "All of their rocket launches have been called off until further notice due to safety issues, called out by astronaut and engineer Jack Carter." My jaw dropped. "And there's more," she said, handing me the phone.

"More? More than that bombshell?" I took the phone and read it, my eyes feeling greedy for every word, reading it aloud so Trevor could hear, too.

"Big news in the space industry today as NebulaX rocket launches have been grounded until further notice. While the details weren't clear on the incident that led to this, astronaut and engineer Jack Carter has further explained his initial general statement that it's due to 'safety regulations not being met.' Now, Jack Carter is making headlines as he revealed there was a failed test launch within the company, which he was involved in. He claims he was stranded in the middle of a Wyoming cattle ranch but thanks to the goodwill of the ranchers, he's made a full recovery from his injuries that could have been much worse. Now, Jack is calling for a complete overhaul of the craft's design, in which the company has put him in charge of. He expects to have a new model in the air by 2028, but don't expect him to be in its maiden voyage. Jack Carter has officially retired from space, a dream he says was never his, but his brother Hank's, who was nearly paralyzed in a one-car crash earlier this year. Hank is on his way to a full recovery and plans to be the lone astronaut on the newly designed craft."

I was without words. My hands trembled as I set the phone down on the table, not even able to comprehend any of it. Jaylee stood up, snatching the phone back.

"I need to reread that," she said, walking over to the couch and studying the article.

"Wow," Trevor said, still holding the bacon in his hand. "That's quite a revelation." He looked at Trish who had a smile on her face. Clint stood up and put his phone in his back pocket. He looked at his watch. Trish got up and grabbed another plate from the cupboard.

"Is James ready for his own portion?" I asked, nervously. Something was going on here. My hands broke out into a sweat. "Wait, how did you all get that article? Why did your phones alert you?" Clint shrugged, smiling.

"There are some secrets of the universe that are not mine to tell," Clint said.

"Annie," Trish said from the kitchen. I turned to her expectantly. While Clint was vague, I trusted Trish to tell it like it was.

"Yes?" I said, waiting for Trish to answer. She just smiled and pointed behind me. Out the window. I slowly stood. My feet felt like they were trapped in mud with how slowly they were walking. From the distance, I didn't see anything yet, but I could hear a distinct engine. One that purred like a classic car. There was someone coming.

I picked up my pace, opening the front door and stepping out onto the porch. *God, is it him? Has he come back?* My heart started to beat so hard, I could hear it in my ears. I saw a vehicle turn a corner. I tried to consider that it was a coincidence that it was an old Ford Bronco that had been restored. Its paint was a bright blue, almost a neon electric color. I loved it. But I still couldn't quite make out the person driving it, though I had a hunch, yet, I didn't let myself feel hopeful. Until I saw the dark hair. My eyes filled with tears. It was Jack.

Trevor stood up from the table and walked out to the porch. "I sent the articles, Annie. Jack told me to send them at exactly 1330 so you could hear the news before he arrived."

Trevor squeezed my shoulders and walked back inside, closing the door behind him. At first, I stood on the porch, still as a statue while I watched the car pull up. But at the last minute, I couldn't take it anymore; I ran to him. I ran to the man that I couldn't deny I loved; the man whom I knew God had sent to me to be my husband. As I nearly reached the car, it came to a screeching halt, and Jack jumped out, picking me up in his hug. A beautiful, black, curly-haired dog came running behind him, jumping around us in a circle. Seven days away from him felt like an eternity—one that God was getting me through, one day at a time, but now I knew I never wanted to be apart from him again.

"You came back." I cried tears of joy as he held me as tight as I'd ever been held.

"I told you I would, Annie." His voice was like smooth leather.

"You did?" I pulled my head out of his neck, where I was breathing in his scent. "I don't remember that." He held me for a moment longer and then set me down but didn't release his arms.

"Before I left. You were in the bedroom. I said that I loved you and that I would find a way to return to you." Every cell in my body rejoiced at his words.

"Wait, what was that?" I asked, and he repeated himself.

"That I would find a way to return to you," he said, smiling coyly.

"No, the first part. I didn't quite catch it." I leaned into him even more.

"That I love you, Annie McGraw, and I am here. I found a way back to you. I want nothing else in the universe. I seek no other galaxy than the one that you are in. I want to be with you. I want to marry you, Annie. I want to be your husband. And I thank God that He brought us together." Tears were escaping down my cheeks as he spoke the language of my heart. *Thank You Lord, for making my paths straight and giving me a man who honors You.*

"Yes," I said, wrapping my arms around his torso, where my head rested on his chest.

"Yes? You'll marry me? Should I get your dad's permission first? I don't even have a ring. You deserve the best ring they make. Maybe Hank could get us one from Saturn. . ." He was cut off by my kiss.

"Yes, I'll marry you. My parents are going to love you, and we can discuss it with them, too. I don't need a ring. I just need you." I heard clapping in the distance. Knowing there was going to be a crowd formed on my porch when I turned around made this moment even sweeter.

EPILOGUE: ANNIE
TO LASSO THE MOON

Jack moved back into the shack next to my home immediately, but Bruno and I became instant, best friends. Bruno shared time between sleeping next to me in my cozy bed, and the other nights he would go sleep in the shack.

Jack was on steady ground with work after his crash. Turned out, they valued life a little more than we expected or at least were forced to. After his crash made national news, NebulaX was on thin ice with their investors. So, when Jack blew the whistle on the miscalculations, they came back with a stack of his reports that were brushed under the rug. Now, with open ears, they were ready to listen, and Jack had an entire team to delegate the changes he needed to make for the systems to be safe. In the end, investors stayed with NebulaX, and some even doubled their initial pledges because they believed in Jack.

Jack's request to work remotely was approved on the condition that he reported to Bozeman once per quarter, to which he suggested we would make a weekend trip out of. He converted the loft into an office and had a very high-tech satellite internet system delivered. Clint was so impressed that he now had cell reception all over the ranch, that he spent most of the day sending Jack alien memes. Jack rolled his eyes, but I knew he loved it.

Jack and I worked side by side in the mornings at the ranch, getting all the hard stuff out of the way. Ever since he got back, he wouldn't let me lift anything that weighed over ten pounds. I kept joking with him that I was going to lose all of my muscle that I spent my lifetime accruing.

"A woman shouldn't have to work in the fields, Annie. That's what men were made for," he said, as he wiped the sweat off his brow and his face covered in dirt. "Now, come give me a kiss." I screamed, running away and laughing. Meanwhile, Bruno ran out to see what the commotion was and jumped up and gave Jack a lick on the cheek.

"There's your kiss, space boy," I said. Life was good.

With our friends and family present, we had a small wedding a month later at the church in Big Horn, Wyoming, that sat at the base of a mountain range. My parents' plane tickets fit perfectly in the timeline, and I was right: They did love Jack. The spring rains had brought an abundance of greenery—or life, as Jack referred to it—to the dry desert climate, and it was a beautiful setting for our nuptials. Pastor John officiated, and Hank and Clint were Jack's groomsmen. Jaylee and Trish were my bridesmaids.

I had always dreamed of wearing a traditional, blue wedding dress—the kind that brides wore in the olden days when they were marrying men who donned swords and knights' armor in castles. My mother had a hard time compromising on white, as in our modern culture it signified purity, which I kept, so we compromised. I wore a bright pale blue dress, that would look white in black and white photos but that still made me feel like a bride. My father cried when he saw it before anyone else, saying it matched the color of my eyes so perfectly and that he couldn't have had a more beautiful daughter.

Jack loved it, too. He said it reminded him of the clear skies on the day that we met. The day he crashed landed, he lost his past memories but saw in my eyes his future. "I found the one my heart loves" (Songs of Solomon 3:4), he whispered under his breath.

And that future is what we are living now, with an abundance of love.

Though we are small creations living in the vastness of the universe, God loves us and will never forsake us, and I am reminded of that daily.

Thank You, Lord, for the beauty of Your creation. "The heavens declare the glory of God; the skies proclaim the work of his hands" Psalm 19:1.

ABOUT THE AUTHOR

Cassandra discovered her passion for writing at the age of seven when she purchased a diary at the Scholastic Book Fair. What began with journal entries about her school and home life later evolved into a collection of poems, short stories, and novels. Her hobbies include skiing, traveling around the

Rocky Mountains, and reading. Much of her writing inspiration stems from her love of dogs, her Onondaga heritage, and her Christian faith. Cassandra's favorite genres of books are Christian fiction novels, Thrillers, and anything British.

She is a full-time writer and resides in the mountains of Wyoming with her husband, Chad.

Find her online at cassandrajoelle.com

OTHER BOOKS BY CASSANDRA

The Chalet Next Door: An All-Ski, No-Spice Christian Romcom

Blizzard Outside. Banter Inside. Sparks Inevitable.

Bubbly book publisher Presley Astor has been told all her life she's "too much." But she's perfectly happy being herself- and taking her pampered Shih Tzu, Priscilla, on a solo ski trip to Sage Mountain, Wyoming. What she's not prepared for is a blizzard knocking out her power and forcing her to seek refuge in the chalet next door...with a brooding cowboy who clearly doesn't know what to do with someone like her. Ford Prescott is a guarded skijoring champion-a rodeo sport where a horse pulls a skier at breakneck speeds-preparing for the biggest race of his life. But he's also fighting cheating competitors and a faith that's quietly slipping through his fingers. As snow piles high and the town shuts down, Presley's joy (and Priscilla's undeniable charm) begins melting Ford's walls. But when old insecurities and misunderstandings hit harder than the storm, they'll have to decide if God's plan for them is bigger than just surviving the blizzard.

How to Fall for a Cowboy: An All-Pumpkin, No-Spice Christian Romcom

She's Glossy Nails. He's Flakey Crust. The Plan? Half-Baked.

In the town of Maple Haven, Wyoming, Autumn isn't just a season- it's a celebration. Ginger Hart is spending the season like she has for the past year: hopelessly crushing on Dallas, the gym bro who communicates in motivational quotes. In her quest for his attention, Ginger's lost more than a few pounds- maybe, a bit of herself. As the town gears up for the annual Pumpkin Stampede, something (or rather someone) rolls into town in a pumpkin-themed dessert truck parked right outside Ginger's salon. Behind the counter? Ex bull-rider Tucker Callahan. He's all cowboy hat and delicious sweets- basically everything Ginger's been trying to resist. When they decide to fake date for his image and for her to get Dallas' attention, he proposes one sugary-sweet condition. As cozy sparks fly, Ginger begins to wonder if God's sweetest plans aren't always the ones we bake up ourselves.

Genre: Christian Romantic Comedy

A Weather Girl's Guide to Love: A Thunderously Sweet Christian Romcom

Partly Cloudy, Mostly Complicated.

Hailey Sinclair had her life all mapped out- until God changed the forecast. Instead of being an on-air meteorologist for a national network, she's reporting the weather in rural Wyoming. Now she's caught between her college sweetheart, Jett Dawson, and Colt Wilder- the infuriatingly gorgeous and cheerful cameraman who seems determined to break through her stormy exterior. Torn between the future she planned, and the one God might be writing, Hailey must learn to trust His direction- and her heart- even when it leads straight into the eye of the storm.

Genre: Christian Romantic Comedy

A New Leash on Life: A Dog-Mom Rom-Com, Book 1

Get ready for a hilarious Christian romantic comedy as we follow the journey of a thirty-something introverted woman, Katie Fitzgerald, who's longing for a husband. But when she accidentally adopts a dog, she discovers that love comes in unexpected ways, and that God's timing is always perfect.

Genre: Christian Romantic Comedy

Fetching Love: A Dog-Mom Rom-Com, Book 2

Three couples, three journeys, and one hilarious adventure on the unpredictable path to love. Katie and Eli are ready to say "I do," but the days leading up to the wedding are full of surprises- especially when Katie's mom's true crime sleuthing lands her in a pickle. Samantha and Mitchell seem perfect together, but hidden struggles test their relationship. Can they find common ground, or will their opposing desires pull them apart? Carolyn and Micah have found faith and each other, but their surprise romance leads to a sudden, life- altering decision. As these couples follow the Lord, they find joy and laughter along the way.

Genre: Christian Romantic Comedy

The Après-Ski Proposal: A Romcom About Love Off-Piste

She came for a fresh start... Not a fake boyfriend. When Claire Riley gets dumped on the eve of her 30th birthday, she's blindsided. A spur-of-the-moment ski trip seems like the perfect escape, until she runs into her ex... With his new girlfriend. Shocked and desperate for a lifeline, Claire accepts a proposal from a charming stranger to pose as her fake- boyfriend. What begins as a simple act of saving face turns into a journey that reveals a fresh start in life and love—the kind that only God could have planned.

Genre: Christian Romantic Comedy

The Curse of Josephine Bagley

Over the course of a century, three individuals are woven together by a decades-old curse:

William, after surviving an Indian raid on his orphanage due to his facial disfigurement, goes on to live among the tribe. But when misfortune befalls them, he is quickly traded away and faced with a pivotal choice that changes his life forever.

Josephine has faced immense loss. Despite her granddaughter's efforts to help her find solace in faith, she finds she can't let go of the past and falls further into her belief that she's eternally bound to darkness.

Saraphina, a fledgling antiques dealer, gets the surprise of her life when a courier delivers notice that she's the last surviving relative of the Bagley Estate. What seemed like a windfall that could help her career now causes her to question her own reality.

In this tale of intertwining mystery, loss, and faith, these souls navigate through nefarious trials to find the gift of grace and forgiveness that extends to us all.

Genre: Christian Gothic